# FIDGET

An Anthology Curated by

Snehal Srivastava



Inkfeathers Publishing
www.inkfeathers.com

Fidget
Edited & Compiled by Snehal Srivastava
Print Edition

First Published in India in 2022
Inkfeathers Publishing
New Delhi 110095




ISBN 978-93-90882-65-6



www.inkfeathers.com

*Featuring the writings of*

Mihika Mazumder, Arundhati Kale, Anoushka Menzies

Ishitaa Shevate, Aeval Maurelle, Kalpana Panda, Shiv Bhargava

Raveena Ravindran, Batul Ezzi, Deepankita Saha

Saanvi Kusre, Suhani Yadav, Syna Mehta, Mahua Shah

Yashashvi Arya, Prateek Sibal, Dev Gala, Advaya Venbakkam

Sharvari Choudhari, Diya Jadhav, Diya Jain, Anusha Malusare

Saniya Gadhave, Arushi Walkade, Ananya Krishnan

## Disclaimer

The anthology 'Fidget' is a collection of 15 stories, 21 poems and 1 prose written by 24 authors who belong to different parts of the globe.

The anthology editor and the publisher have ensured to make the content as reader-friendly and plagiarism-free as possible. Unless otherwise indicated, all the names, characters, objects, businesses, places, events, incidents-whether physical/non-physical, real/unreal, tangible/ intangible in whatsoever description used in this book are either the product of the author's imagination or used in a fictitious manner. Any resemblance to actual persons, objects, entities, living or dead, or actual events is purely coincidental.

The stories and poems published in this book are solely owned by their respective authors and are in no way intended to hurt anyone's religious, political, spiritual, brand, personal or fanatic beliefs and/or faith, whatsoever.

In case, any sort of plagiarism is detected in the stories and poems within this anthology or in case of any complaints or grievances or objections, neither the anthology editor(s) nor the publisher is to be held responsible.

*For all those who find themselves fidgeting*
*as they wait for life to take them their way.*

# Contents

# Meet the Editor

*Snehal Srivastava*

Finding her way in this world, Snehal Srivastava decided to venture into the path of editing and compiling this fascinating anthology with Inkfeathers. She is a seventeen-year-old girl with an insatiable need to pour her creativity out for the eyes of the world. Still wrapping up her final year of school, Snehal is a cat-lover with an avid imagination and pens down her ideas in songs, sketches, plays, poems and stories, despite being guilty of not being a reader.

Snehal took up a theme inspired from her experience as she found herself fidgeting more than often in class. Wanting to know if others went through the same incessant action as her, she took up the role as anthology editor, giving way for others to share their tales and happening that arise from the annoying reflex of simply fidgeting.

# Editor's Note

'Fidget' is a compilation of various unique experiences of different people all arising from the subconscious habit of fidgeting. We all walk our own paths in life and have our own journey. Wrapped in these pages, you will get a chance to unravel yourself in the happenings in the lives of these characters. A wide range of lives present themselves to you, from students to chain smokers and even Medusa herself.

The birth of 'Fidget' was inspired from my own daily life. As a virtual student, I was bound to realize just how much of a procrastinator I am, and hence, amidst the frequent pings of another assignment being added on to my already untouched pile, my mother told me to stop shaking my leg. That's when my brain decided to function, but not in the direction of school. I came up with the concept of Fidget. A portal where people fidgeting away could condense their restlessness into the form of literature fascinated me. And so, the journey began.

The beauty of editing this book was in shortlisting the submissions. Honestly, you can't really go wrong with this theme and that's exactly what made opening my inbox at ungodly hours at night enjoyable, much to my mother's disapproval. I found myself immersed in the storylines and unique thoughts expressed in these tales and made me wonder if these emotions are that of the fictional character or did drops of the writer's souls seep into the story.

I am beyond humbled by the efforts made and the patience shown by the writers who never failed to be understanding of this student-editor's double life. The stories definitely tell a journey of their own, but this compilation, this book, tells my journey. So, I sincerely hope that you, dear reader, who surprising read the preface, thoroughly enjoy this book just as much as I did.

# The Head of Medusa

by Mihika Mazumder

*My nails submerge deep into my skin,*

As my head is cut off and shipped to-
What do you call them?
Heroes;
I see;
They labelled me a beauty once, but no;
Because I am one of my people,
I am ugly,
Hence, I am evil;
I did not ask to petrify;
I did not ask to die;
And as I fidget with this reed,
My anger grows from your planted seed;
You have made me this,
Abandoned me here in this abyss;
And again,
I will say,
I did not ask for this.

# The Raven

by Mihika Mazumder

*The raven outside my window ruffled its feathers with its beak;*

I let it in and watched it,
As it watched me;
Somehow, I could hear it speak;
Not with my ears,
But with my eyes;
It seemed on tenterhooks,
A state we all despise;
Then all at once, it shrieked,
A piercing howl,
The bird had arrived at a crossroads;
To reside within iron shafts made deliberately,
Or to be released into uncertainty?
To be or not to be?
It ruffled its feathers again,
And I watched the raven,
As it watched me;
A mute understanding passing in-between.

# Game On

by Arundhati Kale

*I bit my lip.*

"How many goals will I score?", "How will I perform?", "Will I be promoted to captain?", "By how much will we win?" These were the thoughts racing through my brain as I lay fidgeting, trying to sleep. The sporadic snores of my teammates filled the otherwise quiet room. My excitement knew no bounds. Tomorrow was the day the English football team had worked so hard for. The finals of the FIFA World Cup. England against Italy. The glory of holding the cup in our hands would be decided in ninety minutes. I had to make each minute count.

My name is Ryan Smith, and I am the striker for the English national team. I have, since kindergarten, been passionate for football, when I saw two seniors passing the ball back and forth performing rainbows and other skill moves I was too inept to understand at the time. I aspired to reach and even surpass their skill level, and I worked hard for this goal. Like any other goal I score, I worked hard to manoeuvre my way through the obstacles that stood on the path, finally shooting the ball of chance to score the winning goal. And thus, when I turned nineteen, I was signed by the club of my dreams, Chelsea Football Club. My performance in the season exceeded everyone's expectations, and the scouts for the English team chose me as the substitute striker. I, however, being an overzealous man, worked my way up the ranks. And here I am now, confident as a striker, ready to face the strongest team in the World Cup finals. Italy.

I managed to get four hours of sleep and was refreshed by the time our coach opened the room door, blowing the whistle, his usual routine to wake the team up. He was surprised to see everyone dressed, wearing smiles on their faces. The day of the match had finally arrived. On the back of my jersey was the number nineteen, the exact age I was selected for the English team. I had to make it proud and keep its lucky streak alive. The short bus journey which was usually very disorderly was now filled with the sound of silence. They say silence is golden, but I vary in my opinion. The silence caused more anxiety. The coach, and the man I held as my second father, Elijah Simpson, could sense this. The tension was thick enough to be cut by a knife. He knew talking about formations and tactics would only stress us out more and told us that no matter the result, we would be handsomely welcomed by our countrymen upon our arrival. This thought put me at ease, and the team started talking and laughing as we always would before low-stakes matches.

I looked out dreamily at the sky blue water of the Aegean Sea. Athens was a remarkable city, and I promised myself that I would visit it again. And as those thoughts filled my head, a looming shadow snapped me out of my trance. The shadow was that of the "Spyros Louis" Olympic Stadium, and I was seeing it for the last time at this tournament.

Very soon, we began with our drills, and Elijah with his instructions. The player we had to look out for was the Italian goalkeeper Carlo Tomassi, with an astounding nine clean sheets, and the twins, Mario and Lorenzo Conte, the left and right wingers with a successful cross rate of 59.38 percent and 54.21 percent respectively. They were the main reason for our drills for accurate passing. Our captain, David Sterling, a seasoned veteran with fourteen years of professional experience, motivated us, and a fire burned within our hearts, and we wanted to carry over that fire to burn the Italian team. In no time, we were lined up, and moved into the field, that would be our final battleground against our rivals. I was extremely nervous, as was the rest of my team, but as the sound of the British national anthem fell upon our ears, pride and patriotism filled our hearts, and the fire that was ignited by David blazed into a conflagration that would destroy the Italians. The cheers from our supporters gave me the strength to carry on and my legs, which were shaking frantically, began to stop stirring.

The whistle blew, and our spirits were at an all-time high, and we fervently passed the ball. The passing drills were coming in handy as the passes were short, but accurate. Our stamina was unrivalled by the Italian players and I soon found myself calling for the ball to kick into the net. Just eight minutes in, and this was my chance to score an early lead. This would increase motivation as well as help my nerves. However, these thoughts clouded my vision and the ball went past my reach and straight to the goalkeeper. He gave me a smug grin, and the Italian offence began.

Tomassi, the goalkeeper, passed the ball to the nearest player, which I thought was futile. However, that player was Sergio Napoli. Napoli specialised in clearances and thus, was adept at accurate long passes as well. One long pass later, the Italian striker with jersey number 3 ran like a bull seeing red. It didn't help matters that the goal was red, too. Prandelli ran, as if the wind was on his side, almost gliding now, easily pulling off a 360 skill move, thus dodging our defenders, and moving closer to the goal. A knot of dread developed in my stomach as he inched closer and closer towards the goal. I could see the beads of sweat trickle down the temple of our goalkeeper and my long-time friend, Tommy White. It was all on him. Prandelli made a move, and with all the power he had, he kicked the ball to a corner of the goal. Tommy, in all his wisdom, dove straight for the ball and managed to ricochet it with his gloved hands. He then pounced onto the ball before Prandelli could make another attempt. The Italian scowled and ran back into formation.

Tommy sent the ball flying across the field and yet again another struggle to get the ball through the defenders into the goal began. The defenders formed an iron wall which seemed impenetrable. The defenders did not cave, but neither did we. This was the final match. The match that would give all the glory, especially to the one that would score the winning goal. I wanted that. I needed that. I would win at any cost. The dream of that dazzling World Cup trophy and the fame that came with it enveloped me and fuelled the diminishing fire within. I nutmegged the player in front of me, and turned back for just a brief second to relish the look of surprise on my opponent's bearded face. Passing the ball forward to Caleb, the left midfielder, I saw an opening for a corner. As Caleb ran, I saw Mario and Lorenzo, the twins, approach out of nowhere with eyes targeting Caleb. He had no choice but to back out and pass back to one of our defending midfielders, Brent Schwartz.

Schwartz flawlessly manoeuvred the ball past the Italians and I chuckled. He always liked showing off, that man. Not a second passed and this laughter turned into shock. It felt like the game came to a standstill. The whistle blew and a stretcher came out from the medics' tent. Schwartz's leg looked horrendous and twisted.

The ball rolled and came to a halt at the end of the corner point. It was Schwartz's healthy leg that had last touched it, and now it stayed unmoving. The crowd roared in revolt and the police had to maintain discipline so as to not start a fight between the English and the Italians. The stretcher went as fast as it had come, the only difference being that it had the wincing face of Schwartz and his unmoving leg on it, carrying the burden of not only him, but the entire English team. The attacker that caused this twisted mess was Enzo Topolino, and his actions cost him a clean record on the playing field and granted him the disgrace of a yellow card. Elijah called upon us and we huddled together discussing various strategies, which would now have to be changed due to the absence of Schwartz. A rather hot-headed individual named Mustafa Ali would replace him, and we had to calm him down before he knocked Enzo out, and thus England from the tournament.

The whistle blew again, but this time the reality of the situation had sunk in. All this time we had practiced with Schwartz, and not heeded the unlikely scenario of him getting injured. This had never happened before. Our passing was erratic, and was intercepted twice by our Italian counterparts. We were thirty-six minutes in, and in my dreams, I had already scored thrice. A hat-trick in the finals of the World Cup! What a marvel. But the horrendous injury of our teammate lowered our morale and depreciated our performance. Taking advantage of this, the Italians broke through our defences, and shot thrice. None of them went in due to the patience and composure of our goalkeeper. Our defence and attack were faltering. Again, the dreaded whistle blew to signal the end of the first half. It was still goalless, and we had to make a steady comeback. Elijah called us all together again.

"Lads, I know Schwartz's injury has left you all disheartened, but remember, you should use these mixed emotions of dejection and rage to your advantage. Throw this feeling back to those who caused it. Let them feel your wrath, my fellows! You already know the strategies I have in place for you, and as long as something unprecedented happens, we will win this Cup. For Brent!"

"For Brent!" We all cheered and put down our bottles of Powerade. The English flag soared high in the stadium and the crowd was chanting. The match resumed.

The fervour of both teams could be felt, and desperate attempts from both sides were evident. Numerous times, I almost got the chance to shoot and score the winning goal, but all attempts were thwarted by that wretched Tomassi. My heart sank each time the ball was stopped inches from the line that would mark the difference between victory and defeat. I clenched my fists as if I were going to punch someone, but the punching was being done by my brain. Athletes are known to be mentally strong, but it is only human to feel agony and anxiety when approaching the end of a game, especially when all your efforts have been in vain. The worst thought for me was Italy winning the championship after several long-drawn games with this one being the worst. No goals. Would we move to penalties? Would we have to go into extra time? It was already 85 minutes into the game, and nothing was working. All our practice, all the strategies, all the planning. My thoughts were rudely interrupted by the whistle. As I was lost in my thoughts, the Italian striker had attempted to score a goal, but Tommy's fingers had touched it and it went out of playing quarters. It was a corner. The crowd fell silent. This was the make or break point of the match. And it was in Italy's favour.

Everyone got into position, and waiting for the referee's signal, breathed heavily. The man taking the corner was Enzo Topolino. Hate filled my veins for that man. I despised him. My eyes were on the ball, to ensure Italy did not score, did not win, did not get the glory we deserved. One signal by the referee and

Topolino ran back like an extended rubber band, ready to snap and cause harm. Running forward, he kicked the ball straight behind us all, to the goalkeeper Tomassi, who was mere inches away from the penalty spot, which was an extremely risky play. Unfortunately, none of us had noticed him till the last moment. He was the most skilled with passing the ball, but we never thought he'd come so close to our goal, leaving his own goal open. As soon as he received the ball his eyes went off to the open twin, Mario Conte. However, I saw an opening in front of Prandelli, their best striker, and realised this was all a ruse.

I ran at top speed, yet so slow in my mind. Tomassi passed the ball to Mario, and Mario was ready to pretend to shoot, while at the same time Prandelli ran towards the goalpost to receive a pass and ultimately score. I was not going to allow that to happen. In slow motion, the ball moved from Mario to Prandelli, but unfortunately for them, I had seen through their tactics and I would put an end to this match. And put an end to this match I did. I slid to kick the ball away from the post and outside playing quarters yet again to bargain for more time. However, I had never realised the Italian's dirty tactic. I was the scapegoat. Mario kicked the ball straight to my extended leg at full speed. The tip of my boot that I had loved so much suddenly became my most hated possession. That tip came in contact with the ball, and my expression turned from one of focus to that of utter alarm. My heartbeat ten times faster and I couldn't even retract my leg. This dreaded slow motion was one you see in your nightmare. And this nightmare was my reality, my life.

Suddenly everything went back to normal speed. The ball inside the goal and Tommy falling after a failed dive into the lush, cut grass of that field in Athens.

Tears welled up in my eyes as the Italians celebrated. The crowd erupted in chaos. I had scored all right, just in my own goal. As the whistle blew, we packed our bags. Not a word was said to me. Just sympathetic pats on the back. My coach smiled a rather harsh smile, and went off to his press conference. It was all fuzzy in my memory after that. All I remember is going out of that stadium in Athens and being approached by the press.

"Sir, how does it feel to be the most hated man in England?"

# The Chaos of Our Storm

by Anoushka Menzies

*Fidgeting is a reflex action.*

A passive instinct,
An unconscious response to our reality,
A focal point for our nervous energy.
Every sparking neuron,
Every loud heartbeat,
Every scarred inner cheek,
Every bitten nail,
Every restless leg,
Is a symbol of us pushing through life.
We are a bundle of nerves
Whose impulses never cease to die down.
We don't like the eye of the storm.
We prefer the chaos around it.
That's more soothing than the storm in our minds.

# Celestial Horizon

by Ishitaa Shevate

*I fumble with the edge of the blanket as I lay there*

Looking at the night sky above me
I stare at the triangle the stars have made here
As I admire their artistry.
The stars feel out of my reach
The sky seems like a distant memory
Of a girl that I once used to be
The part of me that lived with dreams
I want to have my feet on the ground
Yet grow tall and rise high.
I want to be able to look around
And touch and see the endless sky
I know I have it in me
To make what I wish a reality
Yet the world that I know loves me
Fills me up with insecurity
I see all my role models
They stood strong and fought their battles

And here I stand in the war field, feeling so fragile
Wondering if I can make it through the constant struggles
And what if I can't catch the shooting star?
What if it leaves a permanent scar?
Should I still aim for the sky?
Or should I learn to be happy where I am?
I won't let my dreams just die.
I choose the star over the ordinary lamp.
I'm going to reach for the stars
And I'll hope I can get that far.
I'm reaching for the stars
And I know I can get that far.

# Conjecture

by Ishitaa Shevate

I see you everyday
In front of the mirror

*Fiddling with your hair*

Trying to make it prettier
But I wish you weren't bothered
And I wish you didn't want yourself altered
I wish you didn't compare yourself
To their unrealistic pedestal
Don't trust the world
It won't show you your worth
The endless beauty of your smile
Or the way your beautiful eyes shine
They only see your divine smile
But not the thousand feelings behind it
They only notice your external flaws
But not the beautiful person behind it
So if you think they dictate your value
And everything that you are

It's time for you to look within
And love the wonderful soul that you are.

# Fear

by Ishitaa Shevate

*I'm shaking my pen*

Trying to think of words
Good enough to spill on this page
Trying to write something unheard
Everyone says I've changed
No one's meant to stay the same
But I fear in my mind
That the old me was much better than the one you currently find
She was much better before
When she didn't worry about keeping score
She never wanted anything more
Than to live her life like any other folklore
And now there's this brand new girl
Who dreams of conquering the whole wide world
She's set to achieve her dreams no matter what it takes
At the cost of everything – may it live or break
I fear she will leave too much behind
I fear she will hurt the ones she loves

I fear she will give up too much that she has
To reach the mountain high up above
I fear that when she has to make a choice
She won't listen to anything but her own voice
I fear she'll ask for a lot that she doesn't deserve
From everyone whose love she doesn't preserve
I fear she'll blame herself one day
For everything they never let her say
I fear she'll have everything someday
But she'll be alone, 'cause they won't have stayed
I fear that the old version was better
For she wouldn't have written this letter
She would know that she was much better
Than the one who now lives in fear.

# Raindrops

by Ishitaa Shevate

I rush out with a paper in my hand
Through the storm to the drenched land
As I sit there on the stoop and watch the leaves droop

*And feel the paper slice my finger as I fiddle with it*

Trying to make a boat to go with this monsoon mood
People ask me why I love the rain
I ask them, “How do our feelings retain?”
The clouds, the heaviness
Just like our thoughts, we compress
Till one day we can’t take it anymore
Our clouds of thought burst and our white skies are all torn
The sky in the form of raindrops
Our heart in the form of tears
This is how everybody faces
All their biggest fears
The raindrops, so fierce and free
Until they’re compelled by gravity
To fall just like the others

Like a caged bird that withers
You feel it on your face
Every single drop you embrace
The coldness inside you
Much the same as the morning dew
The rain that comes and goes
Reminds me of alternating dominoes
Then why do we fear change when the rain truly shows
That things can be beautiful, even if they come and go?

# Tap, Tap, Click

by Aeval Maurelle

*Tap, tap, tap, tap.*

“Stop that!” they say, and my foot stills against the tile.

*Click, click, click, click.*

“Enough!” they say, and I put down my favourite pen.
All day all night,
Twiddle a thumb, twist a ring,
When really, I want is
To quiet my mind and rest.
Test and paper, and tests some more,
Frustration wets my eyes.
Exam and assignment,
I double over in pain.
An ache in my back,
Sleep fleeting, just as sand in my palm,
Head pounding,
Anvil for the hammer of worry.

"Let me out, let me out!"
The shout of the excess frenzy in my muscle,
I cannot run, cannot breathe, not now,
So I go, tap-tap-click-click, tap-click-click.
"Time up, time up!" I hear and scream.
My lungs ripped,
My mouth bleeds,
I am drowning.
'Focus, focus, focus,' I chide myself.
I curl in on myself,
Ripped hair scattered over the pristine marble floor,
Peace, when?
Choose, they say, I am but a child.
My future hangs in the balance, by a thread,
Into a pillow, I scream and scream,
Spare me this, only this.
Not allowed to lash at others,
Not allowed to cant my rage,
Not allowed to breathe, just breathe,
I click my pen and wait for hell.
The kinder, quieter escape.

# The Monster Under the Bed

by Aeval Maurelle

Tassels were such a sublime invention, Leah thought. She wished to thank the person who invented tassels as she twirled those attached to her blanket between her fingers. Releasing a sad little sigh, Leah tossed in her bed for the eleventh time in as many minutes.

Her fingers stilled as something jerked beneath her mattress with a massive force. Curious, Leah peered over the edge of the bed with bated breath, gasping at the putrid sight. Beholding a dark monstrosity of pores that oozed green filth, she flinched as its gleaming claws scraped against the polished maple syrup shine of the wood of her bedroom floor.

"What the—" Unblinking eyes turned upon Leah, blown black and watery. "That's disgusting."

The monster bared its teeth, brown and peppered with holes, and Leah thoroughly regretted ever opening her mouth. "Mannerless filth," it rasped in guttural tones, and Leah watched with rapt eyes as a claw rose to burst a pustule on its mucky skin, the slime splattering the border of Leah's dainty purple sheets.

"This is my room," she whined, as the monster's eyes narrowed.

"Oh, I wasn't aware," it mocked, its mass growing wider and less tall, almost as if the monster had slumped.

Leah attempted to breathe through her mouth when it released a smell like burning sulphur. "What are you?" she hissed, vexed with the monster for interrupting her midnight contemplations.

"I'm a bed-spirit." It clarified unhelpfully.

"A what?"

"A bed-spirit," it reiterated. "I'm supposed to give nightmares to those younger than ten."

"Alright," Leah agreed, finding this no less strange than her usual daydreams. "But I'm thirteen."

"Well," the monster sighed, eyes staring at the ruined floor. "I'm old. Spinning nightmares is a taxing job. You were young-looking, so I was assigned to you. I haven't told my superiors because I like the rest you allow me."

Leah supposed lying wasn't a terrible crime, considering its job. She, too, had cheated in her latest history test; who was she to judge?

"But if you came here to rest, why aren't you resting right now?" she questioned, intrigued by her demon.

"It's all your fault," it exclaimed, its maw gaping in disdain. "You keep shuffling around, and I'm sick of it. How is a demon supposed to relax with that incessant fidgeting?"

"Excuse me," Leah gasped, pressing a hand to her hip. "You're being extravagantly rude. I'm sure a few hours of unrest won't wound you, considering I'm the reason you can even slack off."

The monster issued something akin to a grumble. "You kids are so sensitive nowadays."

With a shrill sound of exasperation, Leah rolled over and shoved her face in her pillow, the faint sound of ominous bubbling continuing in the background.

But Leah's unrest did not quell, and she flipped once more, much to the chagrin of the monster. "Argh!" it exclaimed, raising a claw. "Just tell me what's bothering you," it sneered. "Get it out, so I can finally sleep."

"Despite having all that space under," Leah deadpanned. "Why does it seem you always wake up on the wrong side of the bed?"

For sonic moments, the monster held Leah's bored gaze, until she relented, sagging against the headboard of wood carved with flowers. "I've been feeling conflicted lately."

"Oh dear," it grumbled. "You're having a teen crisis, aren't you?"

Leah scowled, crossing her arms. "Does that bother you? I thought you wanted to sleep."

The monster prodded a claw in her direction, gesturing to go on. "When I go to school, I'm ignored by my classmates and my teachers. At home, I'm ignored. And then I have all of these thoughts pent up in me, things you're supposed to get out of your system through conversation, and then I think about them at night and I don't know what to do with myself then."

"Oh, how tragic." The monster's voice, laced with sarcasm, infuriated Leah to no end. Till it found the good sense to apologize, she stared at the far wall, at a point about two inches above Leah's desk, which looked burdened beneath the piles of notes and textbooks and litter of stationary, the sight looking even messier when you considered the posters of bands and book covers plastered over the pale blue wall.

"You're not making this easy, you know that?"

"Yes."

It mimicked the sound of human vomiting. "I'm… I'm so—sorry."

"Good little demon," Leah crooned, much to the monster's disgust, shown in its eyes as it shimmied away from the lavender coverlets of her bed. "You've spent your life hiding, haven't you?"

The monster blinked in affirmation. "Doesn't it ever get tiring? You know, hiding?"

"Not really," it deadpanned. "I enjoy being left alone."

Leah tossed her hands in the air, at the gilded ceiling fan. "It's no use talking to you," she declared and mourned the ruination of her wonderful wooden floors.

The monster sighed, losing a bilious cloud of foul gas, and Leah gagged on her tongue. Still, she had to admit, it was nice having someone to talk to. "As much as I like lounging beneath your bed… I do miss my peers."

"Did you have any friends?" Leah questioned, propping her chin in the cradle of her palm. "Would you tell me about them?"

A look of suspicious reluctance entered the monster's eyes, but as soon as Leah blinked, it was gone. "One of my colleagues went by Jezeldoug, Doug for short. He looked like a snake with fur, and his specialty was dreams of hellfire." The monster moved its claws as it spoke, and Leah was struck by a sudden fear for her antique light fixtures, its claws barely missing one.

"Lilaltherin had a mass of tentacles, and her vulture and seafood dreams were especially entertaining… Demidorella had large, leathery wings, and made the best burning rootworms. Their secret ingredient? Mortal tears." The monster made a sound resembling a chef's kiss, and Leah couldn't help but smile.

The monster continued. "And I can't forget Jim."

"Just Jim?"

"Yes, Jim wasn't all that bright, but I still liked him. His father made the 'naked-at-school' nightmare popular, and he just stuck with that so far."

Leah suppressed a shudder, having been a victim of that nightmare at a tender age. Stretching slightly, she said, "They sound wonderful."

"Yes, I suppose they are." Did Leah's ears deceive her, or did the monster sound abashed?

"I think it's lovely that you have friends," Leah frowned, collapsing onto her printed pillow.

"You don't need to worry," the monster rasped, but its tone sounded lighter. "Good friends will come later."

Leah shifted in bed, excitement clear upon her face. "Really?"

"I swear on my immortal life," it said solemnly, and Leah snorted.

"That isn't all too convincing… But thanks for giving me your time."

"It was all for me," it quipped, and Leah laughed aloud, surprising herself when she gave a luxurious yawn.

"Guess I'm tired now," Leah smiled graciously, finally allowing the monster some relief.

"Thank the devil," it groaned in reply.

Leah gave an exaggerated eye roll. "It was nice talking with you. I'm Leah, by the way."

"Absintholiam."

With that name preserved in her mind, Leah turned on her side, vowing to stay still. And as she was lulled into slumber by a gentle bubbling, she realised her fidgeting had brought her a friend.

# Security in Me

by Aeval Maurelle

*Nails chewed till the bed,*

The flags are a stain on my wall.
Surreptitiously bought,
T'was a treacherous secret,
Locked in my chest, with leaden lock and key.
I quake, clutching my thumb in my palm,
What would they think,
Of the fragile skeleton
Inhabitant of my closet, beside me?
Hidden from one, hidden from all I know.
This truth is barbed and wicked.
A rip, two, my insides shredded evermore.
My heart beats a frenetic pattern against my frail sternum,
Am I truly greedy, confused, broken?
Am I that base?
A rainbow is born of refracted clarity,
In my soul is nothing such,
A myriad mysteries,

Then a stray thought of desire,
They are tenfold.
Bitten nails against my knee,
I shock myself out of the reverie,
But pain is no consolation at all,
‘Tis a sodden path leads not to the eye,
Of this maelstrom of sensation,
Only further astray, I am undone.
An answer, I seek,
More questions, I find.
I tire, of solving this endless survey,
All I want is a quiet mind,
Security in who I am.
A dream veiled in mist, perhaps forever,
I only sigh in quiet remembrance,
Of a time, a life,
Not plagued by agony,
A hand closes over my heart,
I mourn a part of me,
Lost, no longer exalted.
A tear trails down my cheek.

# The Spinner's Portal

by Aeval Maurelle

Cassia hadn't expected a portal to generate from their fidget spinner. They really hadn't.

The impulse management aid was new, shiny, and everything Cassia could want in personal possession. Shaded black and purple gradient, with vivid red frills that fluttered when they spun it, it was one of the loveliest things they owned, allowing them to quietly stim when their other methods were less viable.

Cassia had expected to become a thing of affection. Not toss them into a vortex.

And in a vortex they were, strongest winds eddying and billowing around them, flashes of garish colour making them cringe, howls echoing in their ears as they clawed at their cartilage, glimpses of scarlet lace seen between the undulating currents of commingled black and purple.

Cassia's arms flailed with little grace as they struggled to find a handhold, their legs kicking futilely in denim trousers. They tried to scream, only to make the horrific discovery that they no longer had a voice, and their fingers encircled their throat, rattling the bones in desperation.

Cassia could do nothing but watch as their form, tossed by the massive gusts of winds, plummeted toward the eye of the storm, a threatening gloom of ebony and violet. Their fingers left bruises on the supple skin of their neck, tore at their favourite necklace of interlocked paper clips.

If only Cassia could speak, call out for help. But who could save them?

A lonely whimper echoed in the chasm as they drowned in the currents. Cassia's braid whipped their cheeks, their arms quaked in the shocking cold, and their nostrils filled with saltwater that tasted suspiciously like their own tears.

A sensation of suffocation closed in on Cassia, and for all their struggle, for all their wretched selfishness for wanting to live, Cassia knew their death was close.

Cassia did not wish to spend their last moments in a scuffle with fate. So, anguished that they could not whisper goodbye to their loved ones nor ask forgiveness for their perceived shortcomings, Cassia exhaled and stopped resisting.

The effect was immediate. Instead of tearing them down, the water buoyed Cassia, parting around them to form a slippery slope, tickling the hair on their arms and swirling around their hips in a warm embrace.

Cassia slid, rapidly enough to send a bolt of live fear straight to their heart. They had closed their eyes, and their path was uncertain, but the exhilaration of an effortless breath and wind undoing their braid comforted Cassia.

Only a small gasp escaped their mouth as Cassia thumped against shifting ground.

With a languorous stretch, as if they had just awoken from a deep slumber, Cassia opened their eyes.

Oh, and what a beautiful place they were in.

The landscape stretched for miles, as varied as it was gorgeous. Sketched into four quadrants, each bearing a unique facet of its own, the grounds took their breath away.

The first quarter was unforgiving ice, darling crystals of snow drifting onto the tundra, refracting a mysterious source of light into a thousand blinding shards that forced a gasp to spring forth from Cassia's lips.

The second quadrant was equally gorgeous, a luxuriant stretch of tall buildings, interspersed with sprawling roads empty of any vehicles. The concrete rose to brush the sky, the muted grey of lovely dusk, a stark contrast to the blinding morn of the ice.

The third was lush green, a forest that trembled with the warble of crickets and birds, the floor overgrown with the verdancy of herbs and flowers, cradled in the dark embrace of night, stars twinkling upon a haven of solitude, where only wild creatures could find someone.

Cassia rose to look upon the last quadrant, a vast expanse of sand that slipped and slid beneath their bare feet. Cacti and shrubbery dotted the landscape, with an oasis of water glittering in the diffused glow of dawn, palms shading the beckoning pool.

But most intriguing was the island in the centre of these lands, surrounded by a moat of black substance, with four bridges of ice, sand, stone and green leading to a grassy plain, in the centre of which a mirror of gilded silver and gold was embedded, reflecting no light, its surface glossy and smooth.

Well, Cassia thought, shrugging to themselves. If this is the afterlife, it isn't so bad. Might as well take a tour.

Heaving a sigh, Cassia strode to the oasis, eyes wide at its glory. The air was thick with the scent of desert fruit and the sound of lizards scuttling against the stone. Kneeling by the pool,

Cassia dipped their palms underwater, relishing the brush of cool currents against the skin of their palm.

They drank deeply, revelling in the chilly wash of water down their throat, closing their eyes to relish the feeling. As it settled in Cassia's stomach, a judder went through them, causing a shiver to run from the root of their hair to their toes.

A slow sensation became Cassia, causing their skin to tighten and loosen all at the same time, tingle and come alive. Cassia was aware of each inch of their surroundings, the rustle of the thick, rubbery leaves of the shrubs, the ripples on the surface of the lake, the sifting of the sand as it stirred with a gentle breeze, the curl of the air in their chest.

Exciting, Cassia realised, rising now that their thirst was quenched. Considering the wood and the fjord, they realised a hunger had awakened in their belly, and strode toward the green, hoping to find sustenance.

Their newfound power followed Cassia, and it thrilled them to hear the gentle, undulating melody of crickets and sparrows, to inhale the clean scent of moss, to feel the caress of the wind that shook the trees in quiet mourning, to glimpse gleaming white fur as it darted between bark.

Finding a wicker basket overgrown with thorns, Cassia cleared the bramble, filling the punnet with wild berries, delicious herbs, mushroom heads, fat tubers, and scattered seeds. Cassia carefully pried frozen sap from the bark of trees and placed gingerly in their hamper the carcasses of plump rabbits.

Aware of the fire crackling merrily in the distance, waiting for them, Cassia settled on a log, spearing the tubers, meat and mushrooms to roast, sucking on a bit of sugary sap to sate the growls of their stomach, interspersed with the sharp crack of seeds between their teeth.

Their meal now ready, Cassia spread their feast on the split bark of a tree, the juices from the meat dripping down their chin, the flesh of the tubers soft as they bit into it, the flavour of the mushrooms skipping on their tongue, the saccharine tartness of the berries dancing along with it.

When they licked the last of the violet stains from their fingers, they stumbled backwards, a hand splayed over their eyes, as thoughts of many designs overwhelmed them.

Knowledge of aeons rushed into Cassia's skull, bizarre dregs of sciences they had learned in school, funny facts they had looked up out of natural curiosity, forming a wondrous kaleidoscope of wisdom on their shuttered eyes, leaving Cassia speechless.

Oh, Cassis thought as they recovered, sitting upright as their mind processed all the tid-bits which were a joy to know. Oh.

A shaky breath leaving their lungs, Cassia tugged at the collar of their shirt to allow the chilly breeze of night to sweep across their heaving chest. Fingers quaking, they forayed into the next quadrant.

As Cassia scampered over the sidewalks of the great city as a rat might scamper in its maze, a car streaked past them, and they peered into the shadowed windows, only mildly surprised to find the seat behind the wheel vacant.

A jilted shout filled the quiet as the sidewalks disappeared from beneath Cassia's feet, thrusting them onto the packed road. Hands trailing over their arms, Cassia jumped to the side as another car raced toward them.

And there was another, and another, and another, and another. Each of a different design, each of a different shade, they barrelled toward them, void of a driver. Initially terrified of the vehicles that left rubber burns of tires in their wake, Cassia found a strange, titillating joy in jumping from the hood of one to another, dodging their darting bodies, like so many insects, with much ease.

Their powers aided them, of course, for they could sense the vibration of the cars' rumbling engines, knew at which angle and what speed they needed to leap.

And at the border of the city, a dizzy laugh trapped in their throat, Cassia knelt against the ground, pressing their forehead to the concrete road, their breath harsh against the painted white stripes, still high from the rush of adrenaline in their blood.

Letting loose a scream of wonder, to rid themselves of this excess, buzzing energy, they made sure to inhale twice, three times, before moving onto the quadrant of ice.

This place was wreathed in quietude, and Cassia hummed as they traversed the scape of cold, the silence oppressive but somehow freeing.

For in the silence, Cassia did not fear judgement. They could do whatever they want, sing whatever they wanted, think whatever they wanted, scream whatever they wanted, could be with themselves alone and still be happy.

And Cassia did exactly that. They twirled in circles, arms thrown wide, ice soothing against the blisters on their toes. They shouted in their tipsy voice, the notes of an old song sharp and discordant, yet warming their heart. They carved the names of those they hated into the ice, permanent until the water beneath the frost found time to wash them away.

They made lofty sculptures and kissed the carvings right on their full, glacial mouths until the glaze melted beneath the warmth of their mouth. They tossed away their shirt, letting the constant breeze carry it into oblivion, and made snow angels, frost nipping at their skin, crisp and numbing.

And when they were utterly destroyed, their machinations having sapped every morsel of vigour from their veins, Cassia took a clean breath of sparkling air, a tear dripping down their cheek at the vastness of the emotion that engulfed them, that sacred sensation of coveted loneliness.

Having explored every inch of this land, Cassia hopped across the bridge of ice to the island ensconced in the quarters, having explored every inch of this land. Resisting the temptation to immediately look in the mirror, they spun on their heels, beholding all that had provided them such jubilation.

Cassia's flesh still quivered with the awareness of their surroundings, mind still roared with the overload of information, heart still pounded with the intuition of action, their soul still spun with the solace of themselves.

Noting red stanchions that had appeared at the mouth of every bridge, Cassia knew the island must be sealed so they could know its secrets. Picking a handful of sand from the floor of the first overpass, they spilt it onto the mirror and watched as the first quadrant disappeared in a flurry of dust. Its power did not leave Cassia, but a part of them still ached to see it go.

Repeating this motion, they poured mud and leaves from the second quarter on the mirror, concrete and brick dust from the third sector, melting ice from the fourth. A whimper passed their lips every time a pocket of land disappeared, and then pressed a hand to their heart to keep it from shattering.

All the stanchions now sealed, Cassia moved to the edge of the island, drawing a handful of black goo from the deep, covering the last bit of mirror glass. Instinct dictating their action, they stirred the mix, until each substance was dissolved in the other, and Cassia could not tell them apart.

With a weary sigh, they parted the amalgam, revealing a sliver of glass.

In it, Cassia could not see the sky, the four colours of dawn, dusk, day and night. They could not glimpse stars nor clouds, nor the eye of the storm that had brought Cassia here.

Cassia could only see themselves.

The dip in their cheek, the luxuriant curve of their lip, their glimmering eyes with wide blown pupils, their delightfully ruffled hair, the charming hollow of their throat, the stunning arch of their nose.

"I am beautiful," Cassia muttered aloud, a massive smile appling their cheeks. "I deserve this."

The words were not elegant, the proclamation not large, their tone not decisive. But it was the truth, simple, soft, quiet, and so very true.

Cassia deserved to find happiness in themselves, deserved to do things they enjoyed, to know the things they liked, be aware of things they loved, know what made Cassia, Cassia. And it was not selfish. It was not unfair, or shameful, or hateful, or inconsiderate.

So Cassia smiled.

Several moments passed in quiet reflection before Cassia knew what needed to be done. Scooping a handful of the dark blend that coated the mirror, they dotted their heart, their eyes, their forehead, the inside of their palms.

Finally, when it was done, they touched the viscous mix to their tongue.

The winds whipped loudly, lifting Cassia up, up, up, up.

Before Cassia knew it, they were at home, in their bed, in their room, in their family's house, facing off a book poster adjacent to their bed.

And in Cassia's splayed palm was the fidget spinner, with its frills and lovely gradient colour, looking innocent, blameless.

Grinning, Cassia locked the device in their desk drawer, and shivering from the lack of a shirt, slipped into pyjamas printed with skulls holding umbrellas.

Fingers tapping against their knee, Cassia watched in awe as they spun crystals of ice in the air as one might spin cotton candy, in their ear echoing the purr of an alley cat as it pawed around in a trashcan, the rubbish belonging to a deli famous for its bacon sandwiches and friendly, grease-caked owner.

Knowing intuitively that their guardian would come to check on them soon, Cassia burrowed beneath their covers, the power of a marvellous secret leaving them restless.

The world needed changing, Cassia knew. The public needed order, reform.

Perhaps, this was the way.

# Paranoia

by Kalpana Panda

*My hands twitch,*

And my nails are bitten
Down to the beds.
I am overwhelmed
By the thoughts in my head.

The world blurs
And comes into focus.
I can't help but notice
They're staring at me,
Or is it all a delusion?

Do you see that I'm not like you?
Is it hanging like a sign over my head?
Do I stand out in a crowd?
Are you laughing at me now?
Every giggle and sneer
Makes me want to disappear.

# Fidget

My palms sweat.
Do you see me fidget?
Do you know I'm different?
I'm paralysed by their whispers.
They're about me, I'm sure.

Who else could it be?
Who's as broken as me?
Picking myself apart
Don't know where to start,
I'm a mess, I know.
Trapped in my own head
My self-worth is in shreds.
When will this end?

My hands twitch,
And my brain seems to itch.
I'm certain they're talking about me
Calling me a freak,
They know I'm different
And they see me fidget.

# A Hurtful Reminder

by Shiv Bhargava

*Clicking his pen restlessly,*

Samuel Horton was in deep thought. Although he was just thirty-four years old, he had been a detective for ten years, graduating from the police academy at the age of twenty-two and serving as a beat cop for two years before being promoted to his role of detective. Samuel was tall, dark and had a brooding figure which most people considered scary. He had handled all sorts of criminal investigations, ranging from bank robberies to murder and petty theft. Through all this he had his partner, Jules Kane, by his side. Together the pair had more arrests than any other detective team in the precinct and they were a formidable team.

Samuel had gone to the police precinct as he would have on a regular day. He hadn't seen Jules anywhere. Finally he put the question out to the room, "Has anyone seen Jules today?" He was met with an eerie silence. Everyone looked at him but said nothing. Mildly frustrated, Samuel sat down at his desk and opened up his briefcase. He took out his trusty pen and opened up a case file to ponder over its contents. He couldn't believe he missed Jules' nagging to stop fidgeting but the seat of the desk opposite still lay empty. He clicked away at his pen, making notes in the case file. A few minutes later, the precinct captain's assistant came to Samuel's desk, giving him a note saying the captain had called him into his office. Samuel got up and headed towards the captain's office. He knocked sharply on the cabin door before he heard a voice from behind call him in.

"Sam, I called to tell you something serious. This is about Jules–'

"Yeah, where has he been all day?" Sam said in his deep voice, still clicking his pen non-stop.

Captain Singh took a deep breath and tipped his cap down a little before saying, "Jules was killed last night, Sam."

A deadly silence fell upon the room. Sam had stopped fiddling with his pen. He didn't know what to say. He couldn't grasp what had happened. Sam fell into a chair opposite the captain as a feeling of helplessness crept into him. Jules had been Sam's best friend for over ten years. They'd had great times together from memories at the police academy to catching criminals and interrogating suspects. Sam clasped his hands over his mouth and said a silent prayer then finally opened his mouth to speak.

"How?"

"Murdered in his apartment," said the captain.

"Who is working the case?" asked Samuel.

"As of now, no one."

"Then put me on it."

"I'm sorry, Samuel, you were too close to it and you don't have a partner."

"Then come on the case with me, if I start to lose it, you can take me off it."

"The answer is still no, Sam."

"Goddammit, Captain! He was like a brother to me. He was there for me when my father died, he stayed at my house for seven months when he first shifted here. Yes Captain, I'm too close to this, but I have to be the one to solve this." Samuel had jumped out of his seat now. He was palpitating and the anger was visible on his face.

The captain looked down in defeat, "Fine, but I'll be there with you every step of the way." Samuel's hands were shaking with rage but he just said, "We leave in fifteen minutes," and walked out of the office slamming the door as he left.

Jules was an orphan and he didn't have a wife or kids; his only family was Samuel. Samuel went out to get his police cruiser ready to go to Jules' apartment. He took out his pen and didn't click it as his hands were still shaking from the news. Sam took out his phone to look at the last message Jules had sent him. The two had been discussing Star Wars till eleven in the night until Sam finally gave in to sleep. He looked at his watch, ten minutes till the captain came down. He felt like breaking down and allowed himself to sob quietly, processing that his best friend in the world had been killed. As he cleaned up, the captain came down and sat in the passenger's seat. Without saying a word, Samuel started the car and drove towards Jules' house.

They arrived a few minutes later. Samuel put on his latex gloves and haircap and entered Jules' apartment. He walked into the living room and saw his friend's dead body. The sight mortified him. There were three stab wounds in Jules' chest, one piercing the heart which had made him bleed to death. Samuel also noticed that Jules' phone had been crushed and wouldn't work, which explained why he hadn't been able to call for help. Sam held back his tears and said with a straight voice, "He's been stabbed so it should be easy to identify his time of death.

"The coroner puts it between two and three in the morning," said Captain Singh. "Forensics swept the place and they didn't find anything except for this letter," he continued as he produced an envelope with no address sealed in a zip-lock bag.

Sam opened the envelope and took out the letter. The letter only had the letter 'M' monogrammed on it. Sam started to think of a list of suspects. Over the years, he and Jules had made quite a few enemies and a few had been released from prison in the past few years. Not saying anything else, Sam took a last look at Jules' body and he returned to the precinct. There, he took out a list of people Jules had arrested in the past ten years who had the first letter of their name, surname or street name starting with M. He then narrowed the list down by only including those who had been granted parole or had served their prison sentence and were living near the city. This left him with a small list of people, so he decided to personally go and pay them a visit.

The first of the three suspects on Sam's short list was a man named Marcus Henderson, an ex-muscleman for the Irish mafia. He had been Jules's first collar and had recently gotten out of prison. At first glance, Sam didn't recognize Marcus, who used to have a bulky physique and chiseled jawline. Now, he looked sickly and wrinkled. Marcus was at a rehabilitation meeting for heroin addicts when Sam came to question him. Just by looking at him, Sam knew Marcus couldn't have murdered Jules. He started twisting his pen in his hand and stared walking towards the next suspect, Madeline Murdock, who was a con artist Jules had apprehended almost six years back.

She had been given 3 years in prison for selling counterfeit artwork to a middle eastern prince. Madeline had finished the sentence without any incidents in prison and had apparently been a model inmate. On interrogating her, Samuel ruled Madeline out as a suspect as she had built herself an honest life as an art consultant for a private collector. Wishing Jackson the best of luck, Sam moved on to the final suspect, Sergi Popov, or more popularly known as The Manslaughterer, who used to be a dangerous member of the Russian mafia. On some research, however, he found out that Sergi had died a few years ago due to cancer. With this disappointment, Samuel started fidgeting with his pen and headed back towards the precinct.

On his way, though, Samuel went to Jules' apartment once more to say goodbye. On reaching, he saw that his body had been removed, but in a small crack in the wall behind where Jules was, Sam saw a tiny piece of paper pushed in. He reached out and removed it and removed the wrinkling slowly. There were two words written on it, 'Magnus daughter.' Instantly, Samuels brain started racing. Magnus was the name of a big-time drug cartel runner who Samuel and Jules had taken down the previous year. He had been accused and proven guilty for four counts of murder and the assassination of three politicians apart from the charges of drug trafficking.

To gather evidence on the case, both Jules and Samuel had gone undercover and infiltrated Magnus' operation. In their time there, Jules acted to have fallen in love with Magnus' daughter who had also been a huge part of his operation. While Samuel had been expelled from the cartel after a fight with Magnus, Jules had stuck out for six months and had gathered enough evidence to bring the crime family down. The jury had found the father-daughter pair guilty, and they both had been sentenced to death. That was why Samuel had overlooked them as potential suspects. Mellisa, Magnus' daughter, had somehow escaped prison and killed the mole who brought down her father's business. He had to figure out how.

He raced back to the precinct. "Where the hell have you been?" bellowed the captain. "You promised you wouldn't leave my sight."

"Sir, I was interviewing the only suspect in the case but he's not important. I know who the killer is," said Samuel in a rush, "It's Mellisa Cortana, the daughter of Magnus Cortana, the drug lord."

"Wasn't the pair sentenced to death?"

"They were, but somehow the girl escaped. I need to know how and when."

"I'll call my contact at the penitentiary and see what he knows," said the captain as he hurriedly took out his phone.

A few minutes later, Captain Singh came up to Samuel, "She bribed the guard and slipped out in the night, but she left a corpse in her bed before she disappeared which led the prison to think she had killed herself. The bribed guard disposed of the second body so we don't know whose it was. He's in custody now, but where do we find Mellisa?"

"I think I may have a clue," said Samuel, "There is a small house on the Harrison Cliff, not far from here which is registered in her name. Normally, the house is uninhabited, but trekkers have reported a light being on inside for a few days. It could be her."

"Take a squad and go check it out. Make sure she has nowhere to escape."

Samuel and his squad, decked up with protective gear, made their way to the cliff where they saw the house in question. Samuel signalled to form a perimeter around the house and to keep their weapons locked and loaded. He then approached the door alongside a second officer. He knocked on the door and as he was about to ask them to open it, a burst of bullets exploded the door. Samuel was able to avoid them but his fellow officer wasn't as lucky.

Sam got to his feet quickly and rolled for cover. Firing a few warning shots, he made his way into the house, but saw a back door had been opened. He then went in and shouted at his men to follow suit. They followed orders and surrounded the girl. Samuel shot her hand, knocking the pistol out of it. "Surrender, we know you killed detective Jules Kane." he screamed. The girl just smirked and said, "I got my revenge, no point of sticking around. Sayonara boys," as she turned around and flung herself off the side of the cliff before Samuel could stop her.

"So she fell two hundred feet to her death rather than turn herself in," said the captain to Samuel, who stood in his office still sporting the bulletproof vest.

"Yes, and officer Dier will be fine, he has bruises and a cracked rib."

"Well, I need you to file the case report and then you can leave. The squad has planned a funeral where we'll induct Jules into the precinct hall of fame. I want you to say a few words."

"I shall be, Captain, but I need some time to myself."

"Take as long as you want Sam, a full month if you need. Just know everyone in this precinct is here for you."

Sam nodded and headed out of the room and back to his desk. He took out his pen and wrote the report, then set it down and looked at it. He then shut it and left it on Jules' desk. He opened his phone and opened a picture of Jules. It was the one they'd taken after bringing down Magnus. Sam smiled and then put his phone back in. He packed all his things and left the precinct, leaving the pen behind.

# Looking Past Tomorrow

by Shiv Bhargava

*Saniya sat on her bed, silently tapping her feet in anticipation and pursing her lips.*

She was staring at her phone screen in worry. The fast spreading COVID-19 virus had made its way to Mumbai where she had been studying. She surfed through different channels, briskly glancing at the headlines of different news stations. They were all talking about the same thing, the virus that originated in China and had taken the world by the storm.

She was an engineering student at NMIMS university in Mumbai in the third year of her four-year course. Having grown up in Bangalore, she was now staying at a hostel by herself. Saniya had set up her room to give her maximum comfort and at the same time be an effective study environment. Her bed was up against one of the walls and next to it was a stool which she used as a bedside table. There was a window on the adjacent wall, opposite the door, under which she had set up her study table. Opposite that she had a bookshelf-closet, a bookshelf in between two single door cupboards. The room was fifteen feet long and ten feet wide, so everything fitted cozily, leaving very little space.

Saniya had two plants on the window sill, which she tended to as a hobby. The walls were covered with posters of her favourite shows, movies, and music artists. On her bookshelf, Saniya had photographs of family and close friends. She also had a few novels which she would sell after reading and use that money to buy secondhand books she hadn't read before. Most of her bookshelf was filled with study-related books such as notebooks, textbooks and reference material. Her study table had her desktop fixed on it and had a couple of drawers, which were filled with stationery supplies and spare notebooks. Next to her study table she also had a small refrigerator and box on top of it in which she kept some biscuits, chips and chocolates for when she felt like snacking while relaxing or studying. There was a laundry room in the hostel building where she washed her clothes and she had to use the common washroom facility. All in all, she was comfortable and happy in her home away from home.

The first thought that crossed her mind after looking at the outbreak of the virus was whether her parents were safe. Both of them were in their mid-fifties and lived in an apartment building packed with people. She picked up her phone and rang up her mother. "How are you and Papa doing? Have you stocked up on food? Did you buy sanitizer, masks and gloves?" she rasped in a concerned tone, without giving her mother a chance to speak.

"Did you get extra medicines and have you made sure your health insurance is valid?" she continued.

"Yes, yes, beta, we arranged for everything. What are you going to do about food? All your delivery apps won't deliver and restaurants are going to shut. The hostel may also stop the canteen because that's where most of the infection will start."

Saniya had a moment of stark terror as she realised she would have to arrange something to make food for herself. Thinking on her feet, she put the phone on speaker and opened her laptop.

Earlier that week, the university had sent an email saying that lectures will be suspended for fifteen days as a precaution and as the situation seemed to worsen, lectures were most probably going to be taken online. Saniya looked for flights or trains from Mumbai to Bangalore. To her dismay most flights and trains had been cancelled or delayed. The prices of tickets had inflated threefold from its regular price and there were no seats available either. Furthermore there were reports online that the government may stop travel amenities from Maharashtra as the state had been hit the worst by the virus, having the largest number of infections. "I can't come home immediately Ma",' Saniya said in defeat. "But I can order an electric stove and some basic kitchen equipment from amazon. I should do it quickly before it goes out of stock or anything else happens."

Sure beta and don't worry about us, we'll be fine. Your father has bought enough food that we'll be good for over a month and we kept emergency food as well. You need to start thinking about stocking up on food and how you will cook it." "I have some ideas so let me shortlist all that I need. I'll call you later, bye Love you."

With her heart beating rapidly, Saniya thought back to when she was a child, in the kitchen with her mother. She remembered learning how to cook dal, rice, roti and a few sabzis by watching her mother. As she grew up, it became a hobby and a pastime. She opened amazon and picked out a few items that she would need to cook food. Firstly she bought an electric stove, a small one with one burner. Along with that she bought a few utensils and kitchen equipment. Rather than buying plates and pannikins, she ordered two sets of disposable plates as they would be more convenient to use and throw. She would have to wash these utensils in the common bathroom but she had come to terms with that as there were no other options. Saniya placed the order and the total came up to around eight thousand rupees. With a major concern dealt with she decided to take a break and take her mind off things. The items would be delivered in a week's time and she would buy the ingredients the following day.

Saniya sat down on her bed with a book. She opened it and started reading. After a few minutes, thoughts started forming in the back of her head. "How long before I will be able to go back home? When will I see my parents? Will they be okay all alone? If they catch the virus, will they get treatment? Will I be back in college for my final year? How will I get a decent placement or scholarship for my post-graduation next year? How will my marks be decided? Will I even graduate?" Her mind was racing. She raised her hand to flip the page but realised she had not absorbed anything as her mind was elsewhere. She tried to read the page again but still wasn't able to concentrate on it. She kept folding the corner of the page in her agitated state of mind. Her mind had been corrupted by the seed of uncertainty and fear. She knew it would slowly take over her resulting in a panic attack. She had to distract herself. Saniya powered on her desktop and booted up Netflix. She started watching Brooklyn nine-nine, it was her comfort show to take things off her mind. However many times she watched it, it always seemed to calm her down. After a few hours she shut her desktop, having successfully forgotten why she was anxious and worried. It was almost midnight so Saniya prepared to sleep. She watered her plants on the window sill and tucked herself into bed. Before she faded into deep sleep her mind started dwelling on the uncertainties of the future as lockdown was being initiated. She was an only child and she knew she would have to take care of her parents in the future. Saniya also knew that her final year of college would make or break that future so nothing should have gone wrong, yet it couldn't have gone any worse than it did. She contemplated worrying any further as there was nothing she could do. Her professors had sent homework to be done while classes were on hold. She was glad she had that to keep her busy. Saniya didn't want to keep worrying, in fact she wanted to use the lockdown to relax as much as possible but she knew she wouldn't be able to make those thoughts leave her. Not knowing how the situation at hand would influence her life and future drove her crazy, as it would any person. As she lay in bed all she could feel was helpless and distraught as the same thoughts ran circles around her head. What if she fell ill? What if her parents are terribly infected? Would she ever see them again? Who would take care of them if she couldn't? What about her friends? Would they remember her if she died? Thes fact of the matter was that touching a single contaminated surface could change her life, not only her life but the lives of the ones she loved. She wondered if it was unreasonable to think the way she was. "No", she decided. She understood that this fear is what would make her think twice before leaving her room or touching something absent mindedly. She knew the following months or possibly years would be hard but she would have to rise up to the challenge of the times. It was either that or succumbing to that pressure and having a mental breakdown every week. The latter was not an option for her. She was determined to take on this adversity in the face of it. With that determination triumphing over her fears, she finally drifted off into sleep.

She woke up late the next day. As she scrambled out of bed she decided to be productive that day and read the book she wanted to the previous day and get some homework done. After 1getting ready in a hurry she started studying for a while. After an hour or so Saniya decided to take a break to read her book, so she picked it up and sat on her bed and opened it. After getting a few pages in she started folding the corners of the pages again, to the point where they almost tore off and wasn't able to concentrate on what she was reading. Her mind was starting to drift to all her fears and doubts again. Not wanting to ponder over them again, she decided to do some more studies to divert her mind. As she sat down at her table, she wasn't interested in studies and she was still thinking about what may happen. She tried to study but wasn't able to concentrate at all and then decided to abandon her attempt after half an hour and watch some TV. After a while Saniya started feeling hungry and looked at the time. It had been almost four hours since she started watching TV. Bewildered, she got up from her table and left her room. She went to a nearby medical store and bought a packet of masks to wear and immediately put one on. It was almost 6 in the evening and the sun was setting. Saniya loved watching the sunset. The way the sky changed colour and the beauty of it all amazed her. Saniya got some shawarmas packed from a nearby restaurant that was open and bought a bottle of coke and went to the roof of her hostel to eat and watch the sunset. Before she sat down, Saniya glanced at the streets. They were completely empty and in a city like Mumbai that was unheard of. She put on some music and started eating and recalling what all she did that day. Saniya felt as if she had wasted the day, not having studied enough or been productive enough. It was all because she had started to worry and overthink, she told herself, and that she would keep procrastinating if she didn't find a way to push through.

She finished up her meal and went back to her room. Still pondering over how she would motivate herself to push through, Saniya cleaned up and decided to sleep early. All she knew was that from tomorrow she would try her best to be productive. She kept her word and everyday gave her best. For a long time she would keep folding corners of books in anxiety and worry. But time went on, Saniya didn't stop trying her best to not worry and day by day she was able to concentrate more. Some days she would be more worrisome and anxious than the last but she never gave up. She would cook herself some food and go and eat on the terrace, watching the sunset and calming herself down, saying it will all work out in the end.

Finally she was able to move past her worries and didn't have to procrastinate while doing her work to keep herself distracted. She no longer needed to fold the corners of books and she was able to read without worrying. She didn't need to keep herself distracted to be productive, she had realised that she had to accept her worries and fears, not be overwhelmed by them.

# Rain or Shine

by Raveena Ravindran

Dingy spaces dotted with tears,

*Tapping fingers to the raging heart,*

Fidgeting through emotions,
When anxiety gushes down the vein,
Encumbers you into implosion,
Pulling you into the oblivion,
Bitter tasting emotions, suffocated breaths,
Rays of hope transpire, they say,
That too after cataclysmic times,
What if this is the end?
Bitterly burning moon peeping by the pane,
Lost broken stars shining pale.
Glistening with tears of agony,
Lonely darkness encroaching
Aches welled up inside, yet never flows.
As emotions prey upon,
I choke, I curse
I mustn't be alive, I wish

Yet painfully I am.
Inch by inch, bit by bit
One step forward,
Few of them backwards,
With fewer smiles,
But, with a lot of hopes
Along with a lot of pain,
And a bit of strength
One day, one breath, one beat at a time.
With a life to live,

This will End

# It's Not the End Yet

by Batul Ezzi

Apart from the ticking of the clock and the occasional hushed whispers of nurses, *all that could be heard was the nervous tapping of a foot on the cool tiles.*

Finally exhausted after pacing back and forth for hours, a girl sat on the edge of the faded blue seat tapping her left foot while aggressively drumming her fingers on her right leg. Her lips were bleeding, an obvious outcome of her chewing through the skin while her nose and cheeks were flushed red and her eyes were filled with fear. The doctors had been in his room for hours and all she could see through the glass pane was her best friend lying almost lifeless on the bed with terrifying machines hooked to his body and the doctors examining him while shaking their heads and writing something down in their notebooks. The silence did nothing to comfort; rather, it was overbearing and it sent chills down her spine.

He was so stupid for not listening to her especially when she had warned against smoking time and time again. She tried to take deep breaths to calm herself down but all she could think about was him. Every time she closed her eyes she would see him smiling, with every breath she took she could feel her walls of strength crumbling down. She promised herself she wouldn't cry and when he woke up he would see her smile but it was so difficult to hold on especially when she had no hope. She placed her hand on her mouth to stifle her sobs. She was a crying mess and she hated it. She hated being weak and vulnerable. It was frustrating. She leaned back letting her head hit the wall. She wanted to scream, she wanted someone to hug her and tell her it would be alright, she wanted to be with him again. She kept reliving the nightmare of fighting with him on his birthday and then just minutes later watching him collapse after a terrible coughing fit. She blamed herself for this; she felt like God was punishing her for saying hurtful words to him. She let her hands slide down her face, her fingernails leaving painful scratch marks on her cheeks but she didn't care, all she could think of was him.

Finally the door opened and she was allowed to go in, meet him. Would these be their last moments together? Was he still angry at her nagging him? Did he hate her? These thoughts tormented her, they made her want to destroy everything around her, to tear out her hair. Taking a sharp deep breath she went inside and saw him for the first time in three days. Oh how painful those three days were, hardly a drop of water or a morsel of food had touched her lips but finally she could crack a smile as she looked him in the eyes. He looked weak and pale but yet that glimmer of mischief hadn't left his eyes as he held her hand and ruffled her hair a cry left her lips and she broke down hugging him tightly while repeatedly apologizing until she fell asleep in his arms. He placed a small light kiss on her head. They weren't just best friends; she was like his younger sister, one he'd sworn to protect with his life. If only he had listened to her. His mind wandered back to the first time they met.

It was a chilly November night and he stood on a wooden platform on the beach, his hands resting on the railing while a cigarette was loosely placed between his fingers. He felt a presence near him and turned his head to see a young brunette dressed in hello kitty pyjamas and a strong citrus perfume. "You shouldn't be smoking. It kills you, destroys your lungs and also puts you at risk of cancer but I assume you already know that so what's your reason? Peer pressure or do you think it's cool?" Her voice was soft yet her tone and her intrusion in his personal space seemed to annoy him.

"It's none of your business plus didn't your parents warn you not to talk to strangers"

"My parents told me not to be outside at two am too but here I am so I guess we all have our rule breaking moments."

"So what's your reason?" she persisted but he only rolled his eyes in response.

"I think it's an escape. An escape from reality because the truth is brutal and not always how you want it to be. Some people do drugs because it messes with their brain. It gives them a fake illusion of happiness even if it doesn't last long but you, you smoke as a getaway from this world but you know there are other ways too. Don't do this it will only make you sick and eventually kill you"

He hated to admit it but she was right and he hated it even more than a mere girl of fifteen saw right through him. He looked at her with a stoic expression yet his eyes seemed to pierce her soul. He scanned her up and down. She looked ridiculous in her Hello Kitty pyjamas and her hair tied into two ponytails. She looked five rather than fifteen but the scars that ran along her hands spoke otherwise. He realized that they were alike. Both of them were broken and trying to find an escape. While he smoked she dressed up as a little child to maybe make up for her ruined childhood, to feel like she was alive again. Finally he could see her cracks too which she tried so hard to cover up. Maybe they could find solace in one another.

"I'm Jay"

"Alexandramist"

"Wow your name is as ridiculous as your fashion sense!"

"Well at least I look cute!"

He smiled fondly as he wiped his tears with the back of his hand. He wanted to be strong for her. He had to fight and he had to live. He couldn't leave her all alone not after he promised her that they would be together for infinity. He looked at the sleeping girl. She was so small and fragile yet so strong. He had lost everything but she had given him a purpose; she had helped him find his dream and taught him love and joy. He caressed her cheek with his thumb.

"Hey you're okay, I'm okay, we're okay. We'll get through this together. You're not going to lose me. In the end it will all be okay and if it's not then it's not the end yet."

# The Star

by Saanvi Kusre

*Clapping his hands nervously on the countertop, he hums a tune;*

He is waiting for someone, that's for sure.
People around him are having a fun time, he can see.
He doesn't care that they can see his restlessness too.
It's not every day for a well-suited man like himself,
Enters a coffee shop such as itself,
A small place for a huge star, yes.
But love makes us all do new things, I guess?
The barista was shocked when he entered,
And she dares misspell his name,
The rest of them would've wanted to remember this moment too,
So normally they would gather to get photos clicked, autographed and framed.
But today… everything is different,
They know something unusual is happening,
And instead of milling around him,
They just observe his tapping.
His legs have joined the party now,

Going in sync with his finger-taps,
Who is he waiting for? Everyone wants to know,
And coffee is just making things worse, you know.
Murmurs of conversation are everywhere,
But the star can only focus on his actress;
No, not the one playing the lead in his upcoming film
Nor the leading lady from the last hit and success.
This lady he thinks about,
and gets a smile on his face,
His heart beats faster, in sync with fingers,
And with his legs, a rhapsody is created.
It's been quite a while now,
And the star is at the peak,
Of his anxiety off course, but even his stardom,
And there's a limit for everything, isn't it?
Seeing that she isn't coming,
He thinks it's time to leave the coffee place,
Five, ten, fifteen minutes more;
Oh! How long for this torture to get over?
He is disheartened, pays and tips the barista,
The conversations surrounding him are now to a minimum
bare,
Every eye on him, and his trained on the ground;
He stops tapping and flees the place – before cameras ensnare!
Cameras and makeup, masks and façade,
Oh, the actress he was rumoured to be with? Well, they broke
up on their date at the Games Arcade;

and while that did wonders on his confidence…he couldn't show it too;
His team had to deal with new issues too…
Still, he woke up and came up on set the next day,
Surrounded by paparazzi on every stage,
Questions about him and her and the night before,
Accusations and curses threw out of the door.
Over the years, yes, he has been trained in,
To keep his anxiety and nervousness all bottled in,
A different face in media and a different front within,
He doesn't know how longer he can stand it.
But this lady he thinks of now,
Doesn't bring up a smile,
Anger, fear, mixed emotions instead,
No one's rejected him in a long time…
So, like Jack and Rose and Romeo and Juliet,
Our star turns philosophical,
His anxiety doesn't improve, just muffled by cameras and makeup,

*And coffee just makes things worse, you know.*

# Solace in Symphony

by Deepankita Saha

Lara felt a tapping noise from where her foot would have normally stood straight.

*'Tap. Tap. Tap...'*

She took a seat. Blaring white lights, buzzing spots and patterns of dark and bright danced on the horizon of Lara's barely open eyes. The hustling of the hospital bay, the slight murmur of the nurses around her and the constant beep of the machines located in the other room hit her ear.

Down below, where a designer shoe would have normally decorated her left foot, was placed a single sandal. Lara had taken it off to ease her discomfort while sitting down on The Chair. She leaned forward and extended her right arm – a response to the vague gesture made by the phlebotomist, a straight-faced, no-nonsense lady with greying hair. The faint scent of disinfectant and medicine was soon overpowered by that overwhelming smell of cotton covered anaesthetic. She felt beads of sweat collect on her forehead. 'Just a mosquito bite', she told herself; and relaxed when the woman facing her gave her a brief, comforting smile to ease her discomfort. 'Thirty years', she thought, 'and still the same problems.'

Lara looked away from her currently outstretched arm, and started into the depths of the purple wallpaper covering the walls of the hospital. Purple. That was the colour of the designer shirt Aarav had worn when she first met him. Louis Vuitton? It didn't matter, now, with Chanel and Dior gracing her closets. And subconsciously, the tapping started again as those fleeting memories swept past her.

Those beautiful curls, cheekbones that could cut through stone, and that shiny Rolex ticking away through time. Time? Oh, how time had passed. She was no longer Lalita Deshpande from the boroughs. Lara Thapar had long stripped herself of those shades. Lara Thapar should have known. Once a cheater, always a cheater. She felt her feet move of their own accord. 'Tap...Tap…Tap…Tap…Tap' It was like she was trying to coordinate her 'taps' with the 'ticks' of that golden hued Rolex. She felt a disapproving hum from the woman who was currently focused on the space joining her arms together. She stopped tapping.

Birthday planning, it seemed. And with Kaira? Lara felt a fresh breeze of anger coming towards her. Stupid, selfish, spoiled Kaira. Sad and depressed Kaira. Lara's best friend, Kaira. Kaira and Aarav. Planning her birthday party. Over a weekend, alone together in Manali. She felt the tapping resume and wondered why she was doing this in the first place. The chances of Kaira making it alive were bleak in itself. She wondered what the two must have thought of that fateful night while returning. Lara tried to picture it all – their intertwined hands, a smile over Kaira's face, Aarav's beautiful eyes looking at his mistress the same way he had once looked at his wife, running his hand over the steering wheel to turn into that blind spot…and then suddenly; blinding headlights, a loud, warning horn, but Lara imagined it must have been too late. And then, Aarav slumped in front of the wheel, blood trickling down his features, left hand still holding Kaira's right. Kaira's delicate and innocent features protected by the airbags that had sprung out just in time for her. A large vehicle swerving around their car and rushing away uphill, away from the mess it had just created. A wave of twisted gratitude fell over the roads of that hill, calming the angry breeze within her. That truck driver – where was he now? Was Aarav going to search for camera footage of that hit and run? Serves them right, she thought to herself.

It was like history repeating all over again. Now, she hated herself for what had happened between them that Friday night two years ago. Is this what Celine would have felt like? Betrayed? She felt this sudden urge to go back to Delhi and knock on Celine's doors, asking for forgiveness.

She was disappointed in Kaira's parents, too, for relying on their daughter's best friend to save their only child's life. A model of society in themselves, putting her in this position. One look at Hira Auntie's eyes made Lara realise that Kaira's mother know too. Lara felt used. Hurt. She wished that they would die.

Kaira and Aarav – together in death? No, she didn't like that. They should –

'Ouch!' The needle pricked her arm sharply, only to be pulled out again. Apparently, there was trouble finding a vein. Lara couldn't believe that she was giving blood to save her best friend's life – the same best friend who had been sleeping with her husband and lying to her about it. What had Kaira said when Lara told her that she thought Aarav was cheating on her? 'Nothing to worry about?' A bitter smile crossed her lips now.

She felt another sharp jab through her arm. The tapping stopped momentarily. The phlebotomist's eyebrows were crossed in concentration, and pain laced through Lara's eyes. Why was she even doing this? She tried to gulp down those ugly feelings pouring through her mind in an attempt to curb the pain.

Pain. She felt pain, but it, Lara realised, was coming from somewhere in her chest – the one in the arm went numb. The tapping resumed, again. She felt herself fall down into a spiral of thoughts, with only the half attempted "music" made from those Jaipuri creations covering her feet, curb her sanity. Was he going to leave her? Where would she go? Back to those narrow roads of Jamuna Nagar? No. There was no way Lara saw herself going back to that small, dark house to face her mother and her taunting. A brief image of Meenakshi, smiling with her husband and their daughter flashed through Lara's eyes. They looked happy. Lara felt jealousy coursing through her veins. Her sister had no right. How could she have found happiness in the poverty of that place that Lara once considered home? She found herself looking into her niece's eyes. There it was again, pain. Lara could never have her own Esha if Aarav left her. What of her reputation?

Salt sprinkled through her wound as she felt the needle finally plunge in. The tapping increased rhythmically. Right now, it seemed like the only comfort in this mess of her life. She reveled in it, and took shelter in its constancy. Suddenly, the room had gone very silent. Why had she stopped tapping? It was like she could feel every ounce of blood leaving her body. That moment of tranquillity gave her a clear head. It was all going to be okay. However, a moment later, however, her thoughts came rushing back into her head. The needle was still attached to her arm. Lara felt her eyes widen in alarm. The sweat had now reached the tip of her chin. Should she confront Kaira? She lifted her foot and continued creating that rhythm. The grey-haired woman said that it was almost done. Lara's shoulders relaxed.

The buzzing noises from the background returned. The beeping machine recording her unconscious husband's heart rate started beating erratically. She saw doctors running into that room from the side of her head. For the first time in her life, she felt unsure of herself. She didn't know what to do. So, she tapped.

'Tap, Tap, Tap, Tap, Tap, Tap, Tap.'

'Tap, Tap, Tap, Tap, Tap.'

'Tap, Tap, Tap.'

The thin string joining the tiny bells attached to the sandals came apart, finally unable to endure the magnitude of force applied to them, and the bells made a jingling noise, seemingly making even quietness and despair seem lively.

The single, loud, ever going beep from the other room threw out all her thoughts from her head. The needle came out of the arm, quietly and deftly, the absence of the thin metal quickly covered by the red liquid that filled its void. The doors to her husband's hospital room opened, and Lara saw the dismayed, bowed down heads of the professionals who had dedicated their lives to saving those of others, step out. Relief that had once taken the shape of tears just seconds ago, was quickly taken over by something else. She took comfort in the tapping. The nurse struck a bandage on the arm, covering the puncture. Lara closed her eyes, but the wetness around them only grew, advancing down her cheeks and dropping to her shoulders like ripples, some of those tiny drops clutching on the freshly applied bandage, claiming it of its stickiness.

The phlebotomist got up, having completed her job. Lara could hear her wheeling away all that blood into the next room – the one right beside Aarav's. The hospital staff had left, and Lara was soon left alone on that chair.

She kept her eyes shut, and willed it all to disappear – click, and delete. The jingling and tapping had stopped too. Lara was immersed in deep thought. The feeling lasted for only a few fleeting seconds. She then opened her eyes, immersing herself in the familiarity of the blaring white lights. It was time to face reality. She got up from the chair, found her footing, and started to advance towards the room where she would find her past – and her future. The jingles-of course accompanied her footsteps and the elevated end of the sandals made those periodic beats that had been her constant companion.

Screw society. She was going to be okay.

# The Shooting Star

by Suhani Yadav

*The incessant foot-tapping had now broken the eerie silence in the waiting room.*

I involuntarily started twirling locks of my hair as my 9-year-old brain went over every possibility of things that could go wrong. So, whilst I knew that I was supposed to hear a soft wailing, I also blamed the movies I had watched for filling my mind with all kinds of apprehensions. What if the baby did not cry or kick? Just like the movie in which it had to be taken out with a vacuum cleaner? Or, what if all that kicking meant that he would punch his way out into the world? Eventually, falling and hitting his head? And the worst of all, what if the baby decided to remain there for all eternity?

As though she could listen to all that hysterical overthinking, my grandmother (ever a picture of calm) put her arm around me and coolly whispered into my ears.

"Try to think of something happy, Suhani. And give that restless brain of yours a little break."

At the mention of something happy, my mind started rummaging through memories from a happy time when it came across that beautiful night that had begun to fade from my memory. But now, as I was starting to settle a bit, I could recall it with absolute perfection.

It was a moonless April night, and the stars were studded into the black sheet. The lights had been put off, and I was straining my ears to check if the whispers from my parents' room had finally stopped after an hour of relentless waiting. In an attempt to nudge me to start, a wisp of cold, fragrant air blew through the tiny holes of my window mesh. And so, I began my late-night activity. When I had asked my mother to get the temple ready for a puja that I wanted to perform, she had raised her eyebrows and gave me one of her what-are-you-up-to expressions. But she did not have the conviction to say no to the adorable mouse-like face I had to put on. I tip-toed into the puja room, clutching my diary with a small prayer that my English Teacher had written upon my great insistence. The incense sticks had already enveloped the room with their spiritual aroma, and the flame sat there majestically, inviting me to ask for

anything. Now, I was not an expert at any of this. But all my Christmas wishes, Diwali blessings and even those tiny hair strands that land on your cheeks sometimes had been spent in asking for just one miracle in my life. So, this was just the same old prayer but sung with unparalleled sincerity and a deep sense of desire.

*Dearest Lord,*

*Although I have good friends,*

*I long for someone who would stay with me from*

*Dawn to Dusk.*

*Someone who would call me Didi*

*And listen to all my tales of fairies and magical lands.*

*Someone who would share a bunk-bed with me*

*And accompany me to the kitchen for midnight feasts.*
*I promise to take care of this little buddy*
*and to be with him through*
*Thick and Thin.*
*If he were to fall sick,*
*then I will take those notorious germs from him*
*and fight them myself.*
*I promise to never hurt or yell at him,*
*But only love and shower him with kisses.*
*So please, send this little guy to me,*
*And I will be the best sister the universe has ever known!*

Perhaps, I was not fully awake. Or, it was the movies again, which were playing with my imagination. But, at that moment, I could have sworn that I saw something streak across the sky with a blazing white light. A soft, warm feeling crept into my heart, and I knew that my wish had been answered.

I was still lost in that memory, but now I was being pushed through doors, and soon I was in a room where I could hear the soft chuckle of a baby. Along the way, I had overheard people excitedly chattering away about the baby boy and that he was beautiful. One would think that becoming a sister would herald a fanfare, crackers would burst in the sky, and birds would merrily chirrup. But this was quiet and overwhelming. And when I finally saw him, my heart kicked into fifth gear, and I was sure that the dramatic beating would be audible even in the next room. Tiny fists tightly closed; long, lustrous eyelashes; soft, supple skin; a reddish tinge on the cheeks and the chin, he was the younger me. But what struck me the most were his dark chocolate-brown eyes. How easily you could drown in their depths as he showed me the future of this siblinghood. How he would fall asleep in my arms while a protective motherly feeling would overpower me. How he'd rush into my room whenever there was a storm with violent thunders and heavy showers. How he'd jump around with delight when he wanted to show me his latest paintings, all of them figments of his colourful, vibrant mind. How I'd notice the twinkle in his eyes when he spoke about dinosaurs, tanks and everything that fascinated him. How we would steal leftover cake from the kitchen like stealthy, agile ninjas. How he'd listen with rapt attention whenever I told him stories of scientists and discoveries. How we'd argue and chase each other in a wild goose race. The age gap of 9 years was a long time, but I could see how the both of us had little pieces of each other, and we could play, fight and confide in each other in an effortless manner. The relationship may remain inexplicable, but I was sure of one thing. There really was a shooting star that night, which set the sky on fire.

# Fight for Her

by Syna Mehta and Mahua Shah

*She stood there, shifting weight from one foot to the other and glancing at the mirror from time to time.*

They didn't want her. Apparently, he wanted to focus on his career and not get married just yet. His family had been so proud. Hers on the other hand, hadn't taken a breath before looking for someone else. She was twenty-five, so according to them, she shouldn't have been working, she should have been married off and have had kids by now. Her only job was to serve her working husband and raise their kids.

This is the mindset of so many of the families.

Even married, working women have it harder than the men, because even though they have a job that is just as taxing as a man's, they still have to bear the burden of maintaining the household and raising the kids, which is supposedly "their job". In many cases, the man never plays a part in this.

A lot of women are not even allowed to work. When they are, however capable they might be, they are not granted the same status as men. Most women are not even granted equal pay to the men in their position. Even the entertainment industry, which is the most popular and one of the highest paying industries, does not grant the luxury of equal pay. So many times, the male lead has been paid more than the female lead. It is beyond unfair.

The basic necessity to get better jobs is education. In many places all around the world, women are not even given the fundamental rights to education. Girls are expected to sit at home and help their mothers in household chores rather than be sent to school. Girls are raised with the mindset that they are not good enough and will never be able to support their families. Hence, they do not feel the need to study, because this has been established since their childhood.

Setting aside their education, girls are not even allowed to live. They are killed even before they get a chance to be born, or within a few days of taking their first breaths. How is it that a parent, who is supposed to love their child more than anything, kills their daughter in their desperation for a son?

Statistics show that over 81% of women have been catcalled, yelled at, stared at, intimidated or harassed online. Even worse, so many have been sexually assaulted. Women are objectified and some men treat them like their own property. They are subjected to comments about their body, which are supposed to be taken as compliments.

Every woman is expected to work on their appearance. They have a compulsion in this society to always look unconditionally perfect, with no flaws. The thing is, society shouldn't perceive these as flaws, because removing them or concealing them by artificial means is unnatural. Why is it that only the women feel the need to put on makeup to look perfect? Why is it that a woman feels self-conscious to have hair on her skin when a man doesn't give it a second thought?

If a woman wants to change herself, it should be because she wants to, not because of the norms and standards that oppress her. It is okay to want to change, but it should be only when one desires to.

One thing that has become very common is normalizing actions and comments, that in reality are extremely degrading to women. Statements like, "be a man", "do not cry like a little girl", "sit like a lady", "don't show so much skin", "women should not be loud", "fight me like a man" and many more are commonly heard in conversation, and the sad reality is, that we do not even notice it sometimes. While referring to an unspecified person, the collective pronouns used without a second thought are he/him. These little things, that we do not even realise, are small but powerful indicators that show how male dominated our society is.

On the other hand, there are so many normal events that make people apprehensive to mention. Regular occurrences like a woman's menstrual cycle are considered unhygienic and impure. Women find it uncomfortable to talk about them when in fact, they are totally natural. We should be able to openly talk about this. Why should it be uncomfortable when talking about changes in the body? It is only natural. Another example is when a woman does not want to get married and have kids. People find it distressing when a woman makes decisions like these. Shouldn't she get the freedom and choice to decide what she wants to do with her body? It is her life after all. Many women have succumbed to the judgement that they have to face by society. It's time the society accepts women for who they are, and not what they are supposed to be.

Feminism, by definition, is the advocacy of women's rights, on the grounds of the equality of sexes. It does not imply women's domination over men, which is how it is commonly interpreted.

Feminism should become a worldwide movement. This is not just a woman's fight. This is a fight for the enhancement of humanity as one people. Emma Watson once said, "If men don't have to be aggressive in order to be accepted, women won't feel compelled to be submissive. If men don't have to control, women won't have to be controlled. Both men and women should feel free to be sensitive. Both men and women should feel free to be strong." We don't need to fall under gender stereotypes. Toxic masculinity too, needs to be stopped.

Women have been treated as inferior for too long. This has to be reformed. Being a woman is not justification for unequal pay, sexual harassment, no reproductive rights and dominance. Merit, not sex, should be the only factor. Women need to be involved in all decision-making processes in every field. Men should not have any authority over women. As of today, many women have little to no liberty in how they decide to live their own lives.

This cannot go on. Each and every person needs to do their part in bringing about this necessary change and it has to be done now.

# Write Your Own Story

by Syna Mehta

*A sharp slice of pain brought her hurtling out of her thoughts as the paper clip she was twisting in her fingers snapped.* She looked down and saw that the clip, reshaped, so now just a metal wire, had splintered, leaving a trickle of blood on her finger.

Now, her tutor looked at her with distaste. "What's this nonsense you've got going on?", he asked with the hint of irritation in his voice. "You weren't listening to a word I was saying, were you? Daydreaming all the time!" He was right. She had been in a faraway world of her imagination, a world that belonged wholly to her. "It wasn't daydreaming exactly", she wanted to say. She would consciously think of a whole new world, for the fictional characters, those she read about and those that were of her own imagination. But she knew that whatever that was, it was not reality. This was. She knew she needed to think about her future. She had a plan, and this was the way to get there.

She mumbled her apologies and turned to the page he indicated, ready for another day of keeping her nose on the grind. But she shouldn't be grumbling about this. It was a choice she had made for herself. This was what she wanted to do. Wasn't it? Then why was it feeling so wrong?

Given a choice, she would have just immersed herself into some fictional universe where she needn't worry about any of this. For as long as she could remember, she had been creating new stories about, well, practically everything. Being a voracious reader and a lover of films, she had lived in the world of storytelling all her life. She had read almost every genre ever written and would practically devour any reading material that was given to her.

These stories gave her a new life, made her feel alive. She would get so attached to the characters, and would laugh and cry along with them, and would almost feel as if she was living in the story with them.

She used to be fascinated by the authors and filmmakers. She wondered how it was possible to create something that meant so much to so many people. Something that made them laugh when the last thing they wanted to do was smile. Something that made her a better person because she felt like she was learning on the journey alongside them. Something that made her feel like she was the happiest person in the whole world. So many times, she would pause her reading or watching and just take a minute to digest how enchanting and compelling and beautiful it was.

Her own imagination grew because of it, and now knew no bounds. She had a plethora of ideas all in that ingenious mind of hers. She had her own version for an alternative ending for a story where it wasn't satisfactory enough for her, she would think of sequels for all the books or movies that were in series. That was when she would actually get attached to the character, after following his or her entire journey through the books, movies or shows. She would absolutely love to think about all the potential these characters had for all the different roads she could take them down. For her, the possibilities were really endless.

She stayed awake in bed every night, not just because she simply couldn't sleep. This was when all the ideas would hit her. A different course of action. All the different directions to take a character when some aspect of the story hadn't been properly defined in the actual work. She continued the stories like that every night until she either came up with another one to work on or she simply wanted this one to end.

The only person she even mentioned these to was her best friend. They had even tried to write a story once. She had so many inspirations for their story thanks to all that staying awake at night. With a storyline, almost complete with dialogues that they discussed amongst each other, they had almost succeeded in actually writing it down.

Today, out of the blue, they began talking about the story they had thought of then. She couldn't help but tell her friend that she had come up with a ton of more ideas and that they could actually finish writing what they had started all that time ago. Her friend then asked, "So you just come up with these and then work on them to actually form a whole story?" When she replied that that, as it happened, was exactly what she did her friend exclaimed "Then how is it that you have got these incredible thoughts and ideas, collected over years, but you haven't actually done anything about it! That's so unlike you."

In all honesty, it was. In any other case, as soon as she thought of something she went out and did it. But now, she wasn't sure what to do. She couldn't possibly write down her stories, could she? They just felt so personal, like they were hers and only hers and the thought of sharing them with somebody didn't sit well with her. When she carried on a story written by someone else, or changed the end, it was based on her perceptions of the characters, and how she hoped their stories would end. But what about her own characters? They, as a matter of fact, were hers. They were her originals, and for all intents and purposes, any book she wrote could only be whatever she wished it to be.

She lay awake in bed thinking of what she had said. She thought about how happy she had been when she reached the climax of the book she had been reading before bed. The protagonist, though fictional, was someone she could truly connect with. She thought about her own stories and fairytales. She thought about her book in the hands of another young child, someone like her, who found solace in these stories. Someone who might learn and grow alongside the character through his or her experiences.

Her eyes flew open. She knew then. She knew what she wanted to do. At half past one in the night, she crept out of her room to make a cup of coffee, and sat at the laptop at her desk, fingers hovering over the keyboard. She inclined her neck and closed her eyes. She took a deep breath and let the thoughts wash over her. All the years' worth of ideas, concepts and visualizations hit her, overwhelming her. Confusing as it was, what she was about to do felt right. Like she had been waiting for this her whole life. You create your own destiny, right? Follow where your heart takes you? Dream big? Most of the best stories involve these beliefs, in whatever big or small way. Even hers. It was finally time for her to take her own advice.

Another breath had her eyes open and her head clear. One step at a time, she told herself. Slowly she lowered her head and stared at the blank screen ahead of her. The cursor was blinking, almost in anticipation. She felt a thrill course through her. She let out a little chuckle, and with a glimmer of exhilaration and a sparkle in her eyes, she began typing.

# Keychain

by Yashashvi Arya

I am staring at the screen

*Fidgeting with my keychain*

Because the thought of you drives me insane
What I feel is unwanted, I try to suppress it
In your eyes, beautiful like marbles
I could see that I disgusted you

I can't hide my anxiousness
Pinching the skin between my thumb and finger
Why is it so hard to forget you?
It should be easier now though
Now that I know that you can't be mine

I am new to this, I feel so heavy yet so relieved
No one notices anything out of the ordinary
My legs would always shake whenever you were mentioned
Doesn't matter if it's now on the news

It's been a few months
I am back to normal now
The essence of your red blood remains on my keychain
And I will never forget what your still warm body and I shared
Before you went swimming in the ocean.

# Inheritance

by Prateek Sibal

*Charlotte unconsciously tapped her foot on the floor while running her finger over the oak leaf pendant on the necklace she was wearing.*

She could vividly remember the day her mother put that very necklace around her neck, saying, "Lottie, you're my brave little girl. You can get through anything." Charlotte wished she could run into her mother's arms and tell her how scared she was. Hearing her mother's voice always used to calm her, but the last time she heard it was a year ago.

She thought back to how it was before her mother got tested, picturing her mother's rosy face framed by thick locks of brown hair, and her nimble fingers tickling the ivories. Was it Chopin or Liszt? Charlotte could never remember which one was her mother's favourite.

It began with small things - forgetting pieces she had played all her life, failing to remember where she had kept the jar of apricot preserve, and being a little more irritable than usual. Charlotte didn't see this as strange - after all, how long can one's memory stay as sharp as it was when one was young? And after spending more than sixty years on this Earth, one is bound to get irritated by small things. It was a sultry Sunday afternoon when she was reclined on the sofa, listening to her mother play one of Bach's Inventions when suddenly, there was a tremor in her hand. Charlotte assumed that her mother's fingers had simply slipped, but a few days later, she noticed another tremor. She immediately got to her feet and urged her mother to see a doctor, but she insisted that there was no need to. Strangely enough, soon after this incident, she stopped playing the piano while Charlotte was around.

One morning, Charlotte's mother left the house to get her favourite - coffee and donuts, from the café which was just five blocks away, but she never got there. The next day, after hours of frantic searching, her family found her walking listlessly on the street outside their house, with no recollection of what had happened. The doctors advised her to get tested, and they found that she was positive for Huntington's disease. From then on, every few weeks, some new loss came along, hitting Charlotte like a tonne of bricks, and she was never prepared for it.

Suddenly, she realised that a woman sitting across the aisle was pursing her lips in displeasure, looking at Charlotte's foot, then at her face, and then at her foot again. She made a conscious effort to stop tapping her foot, looked around, and saw nurses running into a room with a crash cart, a patient being wheeled into an operating theatre, and doctors consulting each other amidst the cacophony of beeps and alarms for which hospitals are known. The chaos almost took her mind off of worrying about her test results, but as she saw the woman's toddler blowing raspberries, she remembered that she was once like that child. How could she ever forget what happened? How could she ever forget how quickly the roles of mother and daughter were reversed?

Loss of memory progressed to loss of emotional control, and then to the loss of the ability to do simple things like talking and eating. Would Charlotte suffer the same fate? The mere thought terrified her. Unfortunately, Huntington's disease does not die with the patient. If her mother had it, there was a chance that it could be lying dormant in her, or any of her siblings, waiting for the perfect moment to emerge. She had been tapping her foot again, but she hadn't noticed it yet.

She had delayed being tested for as long as she could. There was a sort of bliss in not knowing something like this. Every bit of news causes ripples of change in your life and in the lives of those around you, but something like this could cause waves of tsunamic proportions. But where was the person who was going to give her the news? She had been waiting for an hour that day, after a harrowing wait of two weeks after the test. Those weeks felt more like months. It was like there was a battle of voices inside her head every second of every day, one voice assuming the worst, and the other telling her that everything was going to be okay. She had hardly been able to sleep during those agonising two weeks, but they were finally over.

As she looked around, her eyes once again fell on the woman, who had an even stronger expression of disapproval on her face this time. The woman quickly looked away when Charlotte's gaze fell on her. Charlotte didn't see what high ground the woman had to judge her – her toddler was now sprawled on the floor in front of her. She bit the inside of her cheek, continuing to fidget with her pendant until, finally, the receptionist called out her name.

They directed Charlotte to a room where a man was waiting for her. He had soft features and kind eyes, and his hair was only just starting to grey. It seemed like he was being careful not to let his expression give anything away.

"Charlotte Green?" he asked.

She responded with an affirmative nod and held her breath, her heart in her mouth.

"We've received your blood test results. You'll be pleased to know that you are not a gene-carrier for Huntington's disease," he said, as the corners of his eyes crinkled and his face broke into a smile. Thankfully, Charlotte was not at risk herself, and neither would her children be, if she ever chose to have children.

She let out a sigh of relief, and a smile crept onto her face. Charlotte walked out of the hospital, looked down the street, and started going towards the café to get coffee and donuts. As she felt the sunlight wash her face in golden hues, and the gentle breeze tousle her hair, she thought to herself, "What a great day to be alive!"

# The Demon At My Counter

by Dev Gala

I'm standing on a shore
*my toes playing with the sand,*
sinking in deeper and
taking it out, feeling the sand fall galore.
when the waves arrive
I release the sand from the grasp of my toes,
as the salty wind blows
as I look at the seashells thrive.

I'm on the rooftop
dangling my feet off the edge
looking at the moon, now red
as the twinkling of stars stop.

I fidget with chaos in my mind
because I don't want to deal with the demon
at my counter,
waiting for me to no longer be busy,

waiting to tell me
to kiss the earth and embrace the high tide,
and so, in restlessness,
I hide.

# Run

by Advaya Venbakkam

I sat in bed, staring at the hands of the clock, as the events of the past few weeks ran through my head. I, a stellar student, had been sent to the principal's office thrice in the past month. *The teachers had finally had it with my feet tapping and shaking and had sent me to the principal for disrupting the class.* Even though I had tried to explain that it was just a way for me to calm myself down when I got anxious, I had still been punished. Today, the principal had called my parents to discuss how my "anxiety coping" was just an excuse to disrupt the class and ensure that no work was done. My parents had tried to explain but were forced to leave with clear instructions that I was not to be sent to school until I could sit in class without being so bothersome.

I wanted to stop, more than anything else, but it just got much worse every time I tried. Sometimes, I wished I could just get away from my life, even just for a little while, and be free from everything - school, my teachers and my anxiety. As I sat moping, I noticed a faint yellow glow coming from the floor in the centre of my room. I got up to see what it was but before I could reach it, the ground disappeared beneath my feet and I fell through the floor.

When I finally hit the ground, I looked up to see where I had fallen from, but there was no sign of my room. My heart was pounding in my head and I wanted to scream for help but I couldn't seem to find my voice. I tried to slow my breath a little before scanning my surroundings. It looked like I was in a forest but something appeared strange.

The sky was heavily clouded and looked a dark and deep red with no sun or moon in sight and the ground shimmered a little as my eyes shifted between different spots. I looked around as different parts of the forest came into focus. The trees were dark blue with grey leaves and they were the only thing I could see for miles on end. There were no birds or animals around but I could still hear soft sounds in the wind that blew all around me.

With a million questions running through my head, I started to walk through the trees trying to figure out what happened, how I'd fallen and why I had landed in what looked to me like the strangest forest ever. I was just about to give up hope and sit down when I heard a deep, guttural growl. Something was coming closer to me by the second. Without a second thought, I started to run. I am not a very fast runner, and the trees' roots and uneven ground made it even harder for me to hurry. I could hear the growling closer now and I turned to get a look and lost my balance. I hit the ground hard and scrambled back until my back hit something. I could feel the panic rising again as I saw the source of the growl emerging from between the trees.

It was a monster straight out of my nightmares. I tried to get up but my legs wouldn't move. I could feel them rapidly tapping on the ground as I shook. The beast neared and I got a clear view of its face. It looked like it was taunting me, laughing at me, at my helplessness and my inability to move. I tried to back further away but I could feel its breath on my face now as it readied itself to attack. I closed my eyes bracing for the impact but it didn't come. Instead, I felt a warmth inside me, like a small surge of energy had just passed through me and given me new strength. I opened my eyes just in time to see something hit the beast and push it farther away. I slowly stood up, knowing that I had only a little while before it started chasing me again. I started to run again. Even with my newfound energy, which was slowly ebbing away, I was tired and terrified. My feet felt like lead and as I ran deeper into the forest I saw the colours of the trees become darker. The sounds in the wind were louder now. They sounded like voices, familiar voices, but I couldn't make out what they were saying. I strained to listen but tripped and fell. I felt a sharp pain in my knee and I looked down to see a gash. The blood was starting to flow but I didn't have time to do anything about it. I knew the beast had caught up. I could hear its every step louder than the previous. I tried to stand but my legs wouldn't support me. I could feel myself starting to shake again and I knew I wouldn't be able to run away this time. As it came into sight again, my feet started tapping rapidly on the forest floor. With every step it took, I felt my fear increase. Suddenly, I felt a small surge of energy, just like the one I'd felt before. My mind cleared a little.

I heard the beast growl again and my tapping became more rapid. I felt more energy surge through me. The more I tapped my feet, the more energy I felt flow through me. Suddenly, it dawned on me. My shaking and tapping were somehow making energy flow through me. I didn't understand how but it didn't matter. The beast was almost next to me. I screamed, letting go of all the energy, and watched as it stumbled backwards and fell.

I turned and a short distance away, I saw the faint yellow glow again. I could finally leave this nightmare. I could be in my room again. I started to run toward it but I was exhausted. I looked around and the trees seemed to be becoming darker as I ventured further into the forest. The sky had turned such a dark red that it verged on black. The voices in the wind started to become more prominent and I could make out a few words. They sounded eerily similar to my teachers and classmates. I could hear the anger and annoyance in them so very clearly.

"Disappointing!"

"Annoying!"

"FREAK!"

I sat down against a tree and felt the tears that I had been holding in for so long roll down my cheeks. The voices became louder and stronger and began to overlap into a chorus. The beast, which I thought I had left behind, persisted. I felt sick, drained, helpless and terrified. I couldn't run anymore. I couldn't reach the light and I would never get home. My mind felt foggy and every time I tried to calm myself, I just started crying more. I tapped my feet half-heartedly on the ground, hoping the energy would come but it didn't. The beast had almost reached me, but I no longer cared. It was like I was trapped in the darkest room with a thousand voices echoing in my head. As the beast approached, I closed my eyes and tried to think of a happy thought. I thought of the last day of school of the previous year. I'd spent the day outside with my family, running around, having the most fun I'd had in a long time. The memory made me warm inside and I felt a new strength. My feet were still tapping and I was still shaking, but now I felt a huge wave of energy wash over. I opened my eyes to a loud sound that shook the ground. For as far as I could see, the trees looked like they had been ripped right out of the earth, and the beast lay on the ground near my feet. It didn't look so scary anymore. I couldn't wait to get out of here. The yellow glow was just a few steps away and I ran towards it as fast as I could.

As I neared the glow, the ground disappeared beneath my feet again just as the sky started to fade from deep red to a light orange. I hit the surface and opened my eyes to see my room, just as I had left it. My heart was still racing as I glanced at the clock expecting a few hours to have passed but it was exactly the same time as when I had fallen. As I started to get up, I attempted to comprehend everything that had just happened. My knees buckled as I stood and I felt a sharp, shooting pain. I looked down and stared in wonder as the blood from the gash slowly trickled down my leg.

# Mirror

by Sharvari Choudhari

*As she twirled her hair,*
She looked into the mirror and thought,
Someday it will all be alright,
It will be worth it.
Someday I will get to be,
The person I am meant to see,
Every time I look in the mirror.

Maybe the person on the other side,
Can see me, can judge me,
Can spot my mistakes.
The incomplete intensity is maybe an incentive to know,
I'm doing it wrong.

Maybe the person on the other side can see the real me,
Can show me the best part,
Absorbing the negativity.
Maybe it can see,
And know, and understand.

Someday I might understand,
The cause for all the sinking sand staircases.
Someday it will be alright,
It will be worth the effort,
If I trust the person I look at in the mirror,
Who is smiling back at me.

# Human

by Sharvari Choudhari

*She was playing with a loose thread,*
Hanging from her sweater.
Soon, dawn approached,
And bathed her face with sunlight.
All she could see in her mirror,
Was an insecure girl who had stayed up all night.

"Will I ever be good enough?
To be part of a world too unfair?
Will I ever be enough?
To be known as soft from rough?
Will I ever know
The value of everything, or anything?"

"Everyone says, it's a part of life.
The thrill of the chase,
The excitement of the climb,
The terror of the drop.
Will i ever not be scared?
Stop, and just enjoy?"

"Will I ever be enough?
To find one to be my home?
Will I ever be wise enough
To keep what I have?
Will I ever be able to appreciate
My privileges in life?"

That's when a little voice in her head said,
"It's okay,
maybe we are all human."

# Lune

by Sharvari Choudhari

*Celeste was twirling her sunflower locket,*
And smiling to herself.
She lives right across me in the big white house,
With a white picket fence.
She sits and drinks in her balcony each night,
And sings to whoever might listen.

"Hi lune. Can you hear me?
Can you see what I've been up to?
Are you proud of me?
Or are you busy?
Please let me know.
I'll be at home."

Celeste is an heiress,
And she lives like a princess.
She says she'll meet someone, someday,
The date she cannot say,
"I'll be Cinderella and he'll be my Prince Charming
In the middle of the field, he'll call me Darling."

Did you believe like I did?
That Lune meant the moon and she lived alone?
What we didn't know was that Lune was a love's name,
Who was sick and lived in her home.

Celeste bought a sunflower field,
She says it's his favourite flower.
Four months later, she took him there,
On a wheelchair,
When he could say—
"I'll be your charming, will you be Cinderella,
Oh, darling Celeste."

# Closer to Life

by Diya Jadhav

*Rishi drummed his fingers on the window, he could barely wait any longer.*

He ducked ahead, the seat belt tugging across his chest, and asked his father, "Dad, how much more?" His father, smiling at the child's eagerness, said, "Only twenty more minutes and we'll be there." Rishi got back to his seat, his impatient eyes looking out at cars that sped past the window. He continued winding the strings of his bag to his fingers and unwinding them again. Unknowingly, his feet began tapping to unheard beats as he shot critters with his finger-gun pointing at random bikes and cars.

After twenty or so minutes, the car halted in front of a conventional-style bungalow. Rishi's awestruck eyes sparkled at the brilliant blue colour of the house with gorgeous carvings of gods and angels. Compared to his two-bedroom apartment, this vastly spread house seemed like a palace and he pulled at his father's shirt and asked, "Is Grandpa a king, because his house is so big and look, it has a garden and all". He basked in the beauty of the verdant meadow with mango orchards surrounding the house from all directions. The leaves had more hues of green than he'd ever seen. He couldn't help but smile broadly as he dashed into the house to meet his grandparents and cousins.

After about an hour, they were all strolling in the sun-drenched garden. His grandfather showed them all the trees he had grown over the years, the plump pears and chikoos, the towering coconut, the outspread banana, and the fragrant jasmine, while Rishi tied his shoe-lace and got ready to walk through the fields with his cousins. Rishi waved goodbye to his father, who said, "Be careful, and don't go too..." Rishi playfully cut him off, "Dad, don't be like mom".

When they were in the mango orchids, the kids broke apart and ran wildly like escaped animals. Rishi could feel the wind on his face and smell the fresh greenery as he sprinted to the other side. Soaking in the mild sun rays that got through the canopy of the trees, they then walked through a few more fields. Rishi asked his elder cousin Raj, "Will it be fine if I pluck a few" pointing at the shiny black grapes on the vine. His brother nodded, and Rishi felt a sense of utter satisfaction as he and his troupe bit into the juicy fruit. On finishing, they walked off to the maize field. The shiny golden hair sprouting from the corn caught the kid's eye and he felt the silky golden threads. Another kid pointed at what looked to Rishi like a filthy life-size stuffed toy. The toy wore a ragged shirt and had an old mud pot for a head. The eldest cousin proudly told the others, "It's a scarecrow. It looks like a human and is supposed to scare off animals and birds that come to eat the crop. But this one doesn't look like a human does it?" And saying so, the boy picked a rock and inscribed two eyes, a round nose, and a wicked smile on the pot, while the kids laughed heartily. Beyond the fields stretched grasslands where the village cattle grazed lazily, as an old man with a white turban uttered weird cries to urge the goats to keep moving. There was an ancient well nearby bordered with trees, their roots breaking free from the cemented wall. Narrowing his eyes because the sun was harsh now, Rishi saw numerous intricately woven nests hanging from branches. As he looked closer, he saw two chicks in the closest nest, with tiny yellow beaks and tender pink skin that was giving way to new feathers. They understood what the continuous shrill cries of the chicks meant when a weaver bird swooped in from nowhere and landed on the edge of the nest and fed a tiny worm to one of the chicks. Witnessing life flourish in the wilderness was just one of nature's miracles Rishi had encountered. His gaze followed the mother who stretched her wings and was flying back when he suddenly noticed a monkey mischievously chasing her till it got to the tip of the branch, which bent low and landed it on clear ground. The monkey's coal-black face wore curiosity, staring at the kids, and then it scampered up the tree, leaving them giggling.

Strolling ahead, they heard the rush of water and knew they were approaching the river their uncle had told them about. The stream was banked by clear green grass and Rishi inhaled deeply the smell of moist earth. The gang decided to play there for a while and then go for a swim in the shallow waters. It was a sight to behold, with the wonder-filled kids out there, running around with bare feet, sniffing fresh blooms as the wind playfully tangled their hair into a knotty mess. Feeding their cravings which no park in the city would satisfy, they flung their shoes up in the air and their laughter meddled with burbling water was the most beautiful sound, in harmony with the song of nature. They chased each other, jumped into muddy puddles splashing happiness, rolled on the cool grass when they paused to catch a breath, and then played some more. They sang in their clear, gay voices while butterflies fluttered over the river. When they were content with playing on land, they threw their shirts and got into the gem-blue stream with the pebbled riverbed that tickled at their feet. Cupping their palms to splash water, the kids did not think of how tired they would be later. That the daylight was dimming was of no concern to them. They were children, after all, and they had the wonderful virtue of being purely and delightfully in the present. In the backdrop, the heavenly sunset and the silhouette of birds returning home were like the final touches to a most beautiful painting. The soft light of dusk sparkled gold dust on the surface of the river as the sweet perfume of nature lingered in the air.

# I'm Better than You

by Diya Jain

*I sat a desk behind you fidgeting with my pencil at school,*

thought you'd notice how I stared at your perfect hair like a fool.
I always hoped you'd turn around and ask to borrow my pencil,
but you never seemed to need anything and my hopes never fill.

I was twirling my hair round and round,
waiting for you to notice me around,
cause I heard boys like girls who played with their hair,
but you couldn't seem less to care.

I thought it was me,
that I was the one faulty,
but boy you made me doubt myself like no one ever had,
the fact that I loved you so much gave you power to make me sad.

but I realised I'm better than you,
and all the girls you'd dated those few,
I'm a queen and yeah I wear the crown,
so you boy you better bow down.

# The Exchange

by Anusha Malusare

*Her hands were clenching the note and she bit her lip to hold back a scream. Her face was covered with sweat and she looked somewhat stunned, almost like she had seen a ghost until she looked back and then disappeared into the darkness.*

Detective Robert walks in and I'm shaken back to reality.

*I am sitting perched at the edge of the chair, my legs playing their drum; the floor.*

I stare at my reflection on the stained-glass behind him to discover a familiar stranger. "So Mrs. Fernández, how did you know Sally?" he begins, even her name sends a chill down my spine. "Um...Sally was my daughter, Elena's babysitter."

"So is it true that you called her to your residence on the night of the murder?"

"Yes, except she never came that night so we took Elena with us." I said, "Could she have come in after you left?"

"I don't know. Maybe... she did have a spare key to our house."

"So you simply forgot to inform your daughter's babysitter about leaving with your daughter?"

“I umm...”I started to say but was interrupted by a knock on the door. It was my lawyer who went on to confirm my alibi and told Robert that they had no reason to keep me here anymore. Robert didn’t look very convinced but he couldn’t do much with such little information about that night.

Antonio was waiting in the car, I got in and took a deep breath “I cleared it with Robert. Our alibis are confirmed...” my voice was shaky although this wasn’t the first time I’ve been caught up in Antonio’s mess.

“Great, I spoke to my realtor and by next week we’ll be in a safer place.” he said like it was no big deal. I was tired of constantly moving, “But for how long are we going to keep running from them?”

This time he was stern, he meant business. “We made the exchange, it’s all over now.”

It was over but sometimes you must play along for the bigger picture.

It had been about a month since Sally started babysitting for us. I had first seen her when I went to our neighbour’s place to deliver a casserole, a tact to try and warm my way into the neighbourhood. I had gotten good at pretending to be sweet after moving to a different place every month. And then the whole thing almost immediately came to me. When I first asked her to babysit Elena she seemed a little reluctant but agreed after a bit of persuasion and good pay. In the next few weeks, I made sure I called her at least twice a week; a move to get to know her better. I paid attention to all the tiny things she did or liked and made sure to show her that I “cared” . I even listened to her talk about all her boring problems for hours together. I had gained her trust and so it was time to start phase two.

I gave her a call and asked her to come on Friday at 7:00 pm. I made Antonio book our movie tickets as a getaway from our busy lives little did he know about what was coming. On Friday, while we were about to leave, someone from Antonio's past broke in and said he was going to kill us all. They had managed to find us every time, except this time I leaked our location knowing they would send someone. But Antonio didn't know so I played along and yet again pleaded for my family's life. Then I dropped phase three. I offered the man a deal hoping he would agree to this because this was the only unpredictable part of the plan. I gave Elena some candy and asked her to hide in the car. It was 7: 00 PM and there was a knock on the door. I took a slip of paper and quickly scribbled a note. Antonio got to the door and tried to seem as calm as possible. As she spoke to Antonio, I went and kept the note in Elena's room. I came out and gave Sally a goodbye hug and told her not to switch on the lights as Elena was asleep. I shut the main door behind me and ran to the car. I felt the sudden surge of guilt as I saw her by the bedroom window. Her hands were clenching the note that read *"Dear Sally, He came in when we were about to leave. He said he was going to kill us all. Until we told him about you and how important you were to us. It's an exchange."* She bit her lip to hold back a scream. Her face was covered with sweat and she looked somewhat stunned, as though she had seen a ghost until she looked back and then disappeared into the darkness.

I now sit perched at the edge of the seat, my legs playing their drum; the floor. I stare at my reflection on the stained-glass window of the car to discover a murderer.

# New Day

by Saniya Gadhave

Sitting on my chair
Getting so bored

*Playing with my hair*

I'm almost cured
My whole life
I've been blind
The beauty of the world
I never thought I'd find
And all this time
That's been passing by
I've never had the urge
Not once, to fly
But someone very special
Just a normal guy
Saw the hurt inside of me
And gave me his eyes
And now that
I am blind no more

the beauty
I can see for sure
With this gift
Of an angel's eyes
I see my potential
To soar so high
Time to stop
Twirling my hair
To work really hard
And get out there
Need to run
Chase after my dreams
It's a new day
I'm a fresh new leaf
It's a new day
And I'm ready

# Thirty Nineteen

by Saniya Gadhave

Looking up after many hours,

*Fingers drumming on his phone.*

My dear son, my everything
On this day, in the year
Thirty Nineteen
You made me so glad.
No, don't get trapped again
In the deadly web.
Be a boy,
Laugh,
Explore,
Have fun,
Do anything, but don't,
Don't dive in again.
Is that what I think I see
A tiny spark of curiosity.
Dipping your feet
In a cold stream

I see a twinkle in your eye.
Once upon a time,
Every child had the same twinkle.
But my son, my lovely son
You have found what once was lost.
Running wild in the grass,
Soaking in the sun,
My son, my beautiful child
You are learning
How to live
You are becoming a boy.

# Nine Minutes

by Saniya Gadhave

No, it can't be true. I need to find them, I thought to myself. I must.

*I stop shaking my leg and frantically search.*

Overturning papers, and searching through drawers. Why today, today of all days? Just my luck. Today when I need them the most, they have vanished into thin air. I looked at my phone. Nine minutes left.

Oh look, it's the emerald necklace Grandma gave me. My wise and beautiful grandmother, I miss her so much. She passed away a few years ago, on a Friday the thirteenth. The day was filled with bad luck. Bad luck, an understatement. On her way to visit me, she met with a terrible accident, involving a malfunctioning bus and many broken bones. No time to get sentimental. I must find them, I'm running out of time.

Looking through my closet, I dropped something, and heard it shatter. Great, just what I needed right now. I look down to see a picture of my whole family, behind a frame of broken glass. My family being my mom, Grandma, a younger brother and sister (they were twins), my dog and me. I never really knew my father. He left my mother when she was about to have twins, for some women. We don't know who she was, and honestly don't care. I was eleven at the time, and have managed perfectly fine without him. This is all thanks to my mother and grandmother of course. They never let me feel his absence, and for that I am deeply grateful.

Hastily clearing away the broken glass, I check the time. Seven minutes left. He was never late, always arriving on the dot. I groaned in frustration. Ouch! Perfect. A red stream was flowing out of my hand. The glass had made a clean cut through my left palm. Although not deep, it certainly stung. Luckily my first aid kit was right in front of me. Quickly cleaning up my wound, and throwing the glass away, I resumed my hunt.

As I rush into my bathroom, I remember how mom used to scold me for being so clumsy. Everyday something or the other would break in our home, and we weren't a well to do family, so obviously we couldn't afford the constant replacement of broken dishes, cups, and torn clothes. Once, I broke an entire set of China, a brand new one, in front of guests. That was a night neither I, nor my bottom ever forgot.

Putting the everyday scolding aside, my mom was actually a very caring woman. She worked tirelessly every day to save up enough money so my siblings and I could have a decent education. After her regular 9-5 ended, she would go around delivering food for the pizza store that was run by our neighbour, Mr. MacDonald. He called it MacDonald's pizza. Pretty funny to think about, but it did attract many customers. The best part was that we got free pizza every weekend. Although it wasn't the best tasting, pizza is pizza. You can't say no to it. Minnie and Mico loved it.

Minnie and Mico, my baby twin siblings. They were the worst and best part of my early teen years. I was overjoyed when they were born. They were the most adorable babies to ever exist. But as they grew up, they became increasingly annoying. I remember when I was fourteen, I don't know how their tiny hands got hold of a pair of scissors, but Mico thought it would be hilarious to cut off all my hair while I was asleep. And Minnie was more than willing to do so. She later confessed she would stick my hair onto hers and make it long, like Rapunzel. I was one furious sister the next morning. I didn't talk to them for the next month.

My phone started ringing. It was my alarm. Five minutes left. I will be dead in the next five minutes if I don't find them. I emptied all my make up bags, and looked in my shower. Where could they be? And how could I be stupid enough to misplace them. Let me check my handbag.

Rummaging through my black Chanel, I couldn't help but chuckle. My boyfriend of three years, Daniel, had gifted it to me for my birthday. I was super mad at him at first because we all know Chanel is expensive. But I couldn't be angry for too long. We went to the movies and watched the latest James Bond. James Bond, my absolute favourite. And to top it off, he organised a surprise pizza party with my best friends. It was the most perfect day ever. I am so lucky to have him.

Dammit, not in my hand bag either. Where could they be? I have literally looked everywhere. Living room, bedroom, bathroom. Wait, the kitchen. I ran at bullet speed. My microwave showed the time. Three minutes. I am really going to die. Only a miracle can save me now.

I looked through all the drawers, and cupboards. The only things you could see were any ordinary kitchen items. Forks, knives, spoons, dishes, pots and pans. And food of course. A lot of food. My dog Fluffy would be very useful here. She had a very strong nose, and could sniff out anything. Well, I doubt she could sniff them out, but it still would be nice to have her here with me. She lives with my mom and is very old now. Barely moves around. I fear her time has almost come to an end. I can't bear to think of her leaving this world. If a genie would grant me wishes, my first would be to let Fluffy live forever.

Oh no! I can see his car pulling up into the driveway. I got one minute until he knocks on the door. If I don't find it, then no one can save me. The fridge, although highly unlikely, I might have accidentally put them there. As I thought, not here. He is getting out of his car. Thirty seconds. Thirty seconds to my doom. Under my pillow? No. In my shoes? No. Behind the computer? No.

No, it can't be true. This can't be happening. I heard a knock on the door. And the doorknob slowly turned. I watched in despair, and burst into tears, sinking onto my knees on the floor. I heard his voice, his deep masculine voice. "Where are you?" it asked. His footsteps drew closer and closer, my heart started pounding faster and faster. Slowly standing up, I looked him in the eye. He looked back, and started half walking, half running towards me. He lifted his big muscular arms, I closed my eyes and silently waited for what was coming.

"What happened babe?" Daniel asked, squeezing me tightly, wiping away my tears. "Stop crying and tell me what happened."

"I can't find my glasses. I looked everywhere. In the shower, in the fridge, even in my shoes. I can't find them. How am I supposed to see James Bond today if I am half blind?" I sobbed, and sunk my face into his chest.

A moment of silence, and then I heard laughter. Wait, why is he laughing? I looked up at him with a red nose and watery eyes. He looked back down and kissed my forehead. "Oh, my poor babe, she checked the whole house but forgot to look on top of her head," he giggled.

I reached my left hand up and felt them. How could I forget after putting them on my head? I really am the biggest idiot in this world.

I half laughed and half sobbed. “Let’s go watch that movie, and get a big popcorn, I’m starving!”

# Everything is Fine

by Arushi Walkade

[Note from author: This story contains mature content and themes, such as various forms of abuse that may be disturbing for some readers. Discretion is strongly advised.]

*He paced back and forth, his crimson hand shaking as tears rolled down his cheeks uncontrollably.* Jason ran out of the house as fast as his legs could take him, not looking back at the red mess he'd left behind. The brown buildings passed him, allowing him to break into the crowded streets. He put on his hood and mask, trying to mingle into the people, stuffing those scarred crimson hands into his pockets, slowly starting to regain his breath as he muttered to himself, "He deserved it…. He deserved it… He deserved it…" Over and over again. His eyes locked with those of the monster standing at the end of the street, staring at him with those anger-filled eyes and he immediately turned around, walking away from it. He knew he was being followed by it, but didn't turn to see it and instead kept his dark eyes to the ground. At the next turn around the block, he broke into his sprint, running once again, into a small, narrow alley and jumped behind the dumpster, holding onto himself. He heard the monster walk away and slowly pulled out his hands from his pockets, shakily wiping them on his shirt, watching the white slowly turning to red. He stared at himself and began to tremble and whimper once again, finding solace as he began his chant, "He deserved it… He deserved it…" Jason couldn't be made to think differently anymore. He deserved it and it was the truth. Jason didn't hurt anyone without reason… He was the good guy here. They would believe him… They don't have any reason not to. He looked down at his hands and nodded slowly to himself, whispering, "Yes… They have to believe me… They don't have a choice but to believe me…." But, then spoke that voice in his head. That reckless voice that made him do what he did. "Are you sure they will? Isn't it the society's job to make the weak, weaker? The broken, shattered? Isn't that what they do best? What right do they have to even decide whether to believe you or not?" Jason started shaking in fear as he said to the voice, "Leave me alone… Please-" His words broke off on hearing the sound of snow crunching under someone's feet as they walked into the alley. He held his breath, hoping the sound of his pounding heart wasn't audible to the monster walking in. Despite the cold, Jason was sweating and yet, shivering. His hands gripped at his shirt as the sound came closer, and closer… Until there was a shadow over his shoulder, staring down at him. Jason didn't dare to look up, but he knew it was the blue monster. It had to be. Jason could feel his heart in his throat, pounding away like it was the last time it would beat. He waited with his entire body frozen for the hits to fall on his body, but instead a gentle hand lay on his cheek.

Jason's eyes snapped open and he lay there on his bed, taking deep shaky breaths. It was just a dream… Or maybe this is. The dream doesn't seem any better than this nightmare he lives in. He got out of bed, limping to his mirror and stared at his bruised face, sighing in relief when he heard his uncle's car drive away. He covered up his wounds, put on thick clothes, covering every inch of his skin, despite it being the middle of June, before putting on a smile and setting out for another day at school… Another day, in this living nightmare. Another day of his pretence that everything is fine.

# Rhapsody of Regret

by Ananya Krishnan

*Her jean-clad knee bounced nervously, her heels tapping out a staccato rhythm that she had long forgotten the melody to.*

She anxiously glanced at the person occupying the seat in front of her, taking in the distant gaze and the defensive posture, their shuttered expression hurting her a bit more than she'd like to admit.

The quiet was stifling, suffocating her more than the monsoon air outside. She drummed her manicured nails on the Styrofoam cup nestled in her hands, the beat complementing the one her feet were tapping, a perfect counter-melody. She couldn't for the life of her remember the song.

"It's, erm, been a while," she finally offered, hesitantly breaking the awkward silence that had descended upon the table.

"Yeah."

"How- how have you been?" She nervously glimpsed at the table.

A pause. "Good. Busy."

"Oh, that's nice!" she smiled softly, her heart hammering in her chest.

Her companion merely stared, sipping a large cup of coffee with a blank gaze.

"Uhm, the weather's nice, isn't it?" she said, desperate enough for conversation to resort to small talk about the damn weather. What had they come to?

"Sure."

A lone tear escaped her cheek before she knew what was happening, and she hurriedly flicked it off, rubbing at her face furiously, horrifically embarrassed.

The stony gaze on her softened imperceptibly. "Might rain soon, right?"

She grasped the meagre sentence for what it was, an olive branch of the kindest, most generous variety, and jumped on it. "Yeah, yeah," she smiled shakily, "You'll have to take out your yellow raincoat soon, huh?"

Those familiar brown eyes framed by the slightest smudge of black sharpened again, the shutters that had opened up almost indiscernible out of pity slamming back down with a cold, metallic bang.

God, why was she so stupid? Why did she say that?

The silence that settled over the table now was heavy, accusatory, wrapping a foreign hand around her heart and squeezing it with vengeance. She couldn't say that she didn't deserve it.

"I'm sorry," she whispered, her eyes welling up. She was pathetic, wasn't she? Forcing someone whose heart she'd mercilessly stomped on to meet her for coffee, as if they could

ever overcome the gaping chasm she'd put between them and pretend it was all dandy and talk about the stupid weather.

"You should be."

It was cool inside the cafe, the sleek air conditioning turned up as welcome respite from the sweltering humidity of June, but the tears that rolled down her cheeks were hot, scorching, leaving a trail of burning regret in their wake. She didn't think she could speak even if she tried.

Another pregnant pause. "I shouldn't have said that, I apologise."

"No, no," she frantically sought to reply, her throat clogged up, "I deserve it. You- you can say whatever you want, I'll deserve it."

A derisive scoff. "You'll deserve it alright, but I don't want to insult you. That makes me as bad as you are."

That stung, the matter-of-fact words burning her heart more than anything that she had heard about herself before. She wanted to sob, the heart-wrenching, tear-draining, loudly yelling kind, but she didn't think anyone, least of all her companion, would appreciate her theatrics. She heaved a shaky breath, desperately trying not to break down in the middle of the campus cafe.

"Why did you call me here?" Bitter, muted rage coated the words and they were pained, as if it had taken great effort just to speak them.

Her eyes snapped to her companion's face, the sweet burn of guilt colouring her face red as she took in the indifferent yet tortured look in their eyes. Saying that she had just wanted to apologise would be a lie, one that she didn't think she could say with a straight face, not without giving up her secret- that she was still stupidly, overwhelmingly in love, that she wanted them back.

Another cutting scoff sounded at her silence, one that sounded much angrier. "You want me back, don't you?"

She couldn't bring herself to meet their gaze, flushing in shame as her finger traced the curves of her name written on her coffee cup.

"What, you realised that your life is so incredibly boring without me, did you?" Her companion put down their coffee cup with a muffled thump, offense straightening their posture in the plush chair. "Now that you know that I'm interesting enough, you want me back?"

She shrunk further and further into the chair, the tight seam of her sleeves cutting painfully into her arms as her shoulders hunched together in reproach.

"Get one thing straight," they bit out, their eyes wild and sparking in fury, the most expressive she had seen them ever since that day she had told them that she wasn't in love anymore, the alcohol in her system muddling her mind. "You don't deserve to want me back, hell, you don't even deserve to breathe in my vicinity after everything that you've said."

She whimpered.

"I can't believe I agreed to this stupid meeting," they muttered after looking at her pathetic form, brushing off the lint from their pants as they stood up. "Don't call me, understand? I don't want to see you again."

She was helpless to do anything but watch as they stalked out of the cafe, staring forlornly at the lithe movements of their figure as they walked out of her life without sparing her a second glance.

The hurt she felt was all-consuming, pain filling her body to the brim till it started spilling from her eyes again, burning paths down her cheek as her mind tortured her with a film reel of everything that she had done wrong, rewinding and pausing at the exact moment her sharp words had hit her lover, when all had been lost.

God, how did she have the audacity to call them and think of asking them for a second chance, when the scars she had left behind had barely scabbed over? Time had scarcely healed the wounds of her drunk lashing, and she dared ask them out for coffee in the very cafe where they had met? She was a fool. A stupid, lovesick fool.

"Ma'am, will you be needing anything else?" A worker awkwardly voiced in the midst of her self-pity party, their eyes filled with sympathy, no doubt at her woeful state of being.

"No, no," she sniffled, delicately wiping the tears off her face with an embroidered handkerchief, stuffing it in her handbag before standing up from her seat, taking her coffee in hand. "I'm just leaving," she attempted to muster up a smile, not quite sure if it hit the mark.

As she weaved in between tables to reach the exit, her ears caught a stray melody that another patron was humming, her heart jumping when she realised that it was the forgotten tune she had been tapping out. Lyrics intertwined themselves with the beat and the melody, her mind conjuring up the words seemingly out of nowhere, and she smiled in resignation when their meaning sunk in.

It was a song of regret.

# Meet the Co-Authors

**Mihika Mazumder**

Mihika Mazumder is a fourteen-year-old aspiring writer and artist. She recently published a website called Persephone's Portfolio to showcase these works. Mihika is also a musician who enjoys playing the guitar, violin, and the kalimba. 'The Raven', inspired by Edgar Allan Poe's poem of the same name, is a conversation between a person and their mind which is frightened at having been given a choice to be free or to remain within its cage. 'The Head of Medusa' explores the justified rage-filled thoughts of Medusa. She harbours hatred for her enemies only because of their own cold-blooded hearts, and eyes clouded by society's perceptions. You can write to her at: mihikamazumder18@gmail.com

**Arundhati Kale**

Arundhati Kale is twenty years old. Studying in St. Mary's Junior College, she plays the drums and begs her vice principal to start the school band every day. Arundhati enjoys music, especially classic rock and metal. She loves eating, especially instant noodles which she can cook in two minutes instead of five.

**Ishitaa Shevate**

Ishitaa is a fifteen-year-old girl currently studying at St. Mary's Junior College. Music and dance have been a part of her for as long as she can remember, and she picked up writing when she

was eleven years old. She loves playing the piano and guitar. Her muse lies in what she sees around her – what she studies, the people in her life, things she watches, and music she listens to. She likes the thrill of trying to portray an emotion with exactitude, she enjoys how her mind has to work for getting the perfect words to describe what she wants to say. She dreams of being a singer-songwriter and trying to make this world a better place.

You can listen to her songs on her YouTube channel 'Ishitaa Shevate'. You can connect with her on Instagram @ishitaashevate and email her at ishitaa.shevate17@gmail.com.

**Anoushka Menzies**

Anoushka Menzies is an eighteen-year-old aspiring biotechnology student, whose poetry and artwork is steeped in nature and biology metaphors. The symmetry and asymmetry in nature intrigues her and inspires her to learn how to adapt to the ever-evolving lessons of life. A budding artist, she dabbles in many mediums, and she also is an eclectic violinist. You can find her artwork on Instagram @spiraling.into.art

**Aeval Maurelle**

Aeval Maurelle is the moniker given to themselves by Savni Apte, who are currently studying at The Bishops Junior College, Pune.

They have been writing since the age of eight and are currently working on an original novel. They aspire to become an engineer.

The poem "Tap, Tap, Click, Click" expands on the themes of students struggling to cope with the pressures of academic life, and how often one feels as if one is trapped in a never-ending cycle. The poem "Security In Me" explores Aeval's inner conflict, how the emotion of self-doubt arises strongly in times of conflict, perhaps when one is keeping a life altering secret. "The Monster Under The Bed" is a piece of work reflective of the idea that friends can be made in the unlikeliest of places, and that one must only look.

"The Spinner's Portal" is a short story taking place outside our known reality, with the primary message that loving the companionship of yourself is the greatest bliss of all.

**Kalpana Panda**

Kalpana Panda is an avid bibliophile who loves to write in her spare time. She is currently studying in the Bishop's Junior College, Camp, Pune. She has an ardent interest in quizzing, maths, logic and the Sciences, especially robotics. Kalpana is also a passionate advocate for human rights, equality for ostracised and marginalised communities, as well as gender equality, and hopes to bring about change in the world through her writings. Her hobbies include music, chess and simply curling up on a couch with a good book. You can write to Kalpana at kalpspanda@gmail.com.

**Shiv Bhargava**

Shiv Bhargava is a seventeen-year-old alumnus of St. Mary's School Mumbai. Growing up, Shiv loved exploring lands far away in books and developed a hobby writing about such places himself. Currently, he is aspiring to become an engineer and is studying towards this dream at PACE Junior College, Mumbai.

"A Hurtful Reminder" is a story about a police detective who suffers the loss of his best friend and is now solving the case of their murder. It showcases the different emotions that one deals with during the loss of a close friend. You can write to Shiv at shiv.bhargava2213@gmail.com.

**Raveena Ravindran**

Raveena is a restless twenty-three-year-old and is currently pursuing her Master's in Journalism. She is a full-time dreamer and a part-time writer. Writing is the one thing which acts as her solace, escape, and that keeps her going. She always looks forward for food and a good read.

"Rain and Shine" is a poem about that vulnerable state which nobody talks about: Verses from that part of the day where one crumbles on to the cold floor; about those moments which don't kill but make one stronger. This poem is an ode to all those who fight those lone battles with themselves. You can contact her on raveenar2@gmail.com.

**Batul Ezzi**

Batul Ezzi is a seventeen-year-old girl who studies in St. Mary's Junior College. Her short stories focus mostly on friendship, family relations and death, and she aspires to be a famous author one day. She is also a great cook who loves experimenting with food and she loves to sing. Her favourite songs are from the Disney franchise and Korean pop. "It's Not the End Yet" is a short story about two teenagers who come from broken homes and look for an escape, until they meet and find solace in each other. You can connect with her via Instagram @never_too.much_to.try and write an email to her at batul.ezzi17@gmail.com.

**Saanvi Kusre**

Saanvi is an eighteen-year-old girl pursuing Mechanical Engineering in Mumbai. She has always liked creative writing, and poems and short stories are her forte. She is inclined towards telling different stories through her poems, and tries to do something new in each piece that she writes.

You can reach out to her at saanvirkusre@gmail.com.

"The Star" is about a person who is an actor to the world, but wants everyone to know that he is a human, too. He can also have problems that are hard to battle like a common man, but with his position and status, he has to keep it all to himself. My poem picks his story when he decides to meet someone at a public place. The question is, what happens after?

**Deepankita Saha**

Deepankita is a seventeen-year-old girl who is currently studying at The Orbis School, Pune. She finds writing comforting and draws inspiration from her daily experiences. Besides being a procrastinator and ambivert, she loves reading and drawing, and is a trained Bharatnatyam dancer. You can write to her at deepankitas2017@gmail.com.

**Suhani Yadav**

Suhani is currently a student at Army Public School, Pune. She had always relied on art as an escape from the mundane routine of life, until she started writing articles for her art blog. Only then she realised what a profound and beautiful medium of expression writing was, and found solace in the combination of art and writing. Her hobbies include photography and painting/designing. Apart from this, she has immense interest in science and technology and hopes to become a software engineer. You can write to her at suhaniyadav590@gmail.com.

**Syna Mehta and Mahua Shah**

Syna is a seventeen-yea-old girl who completed her schooling at the St. Mary's School, Pune. She is a logophile and a voracious reader who loves writing or anything to do with words and the language. She is fascinated by authors and how they bring characters to life on their pages.

Mahua Shah is a seventeen-year-old girl who is currently studying in The Bishop's School, Pune. She enjoys reading, and loves to bake. She spends her free time in the enchanted world of a book or outdoors in the sun. She has never really had a specific interest in writing but enjoys it once in a while. She can be contacted at mahuaashah@gmail.com.

"Fight for Her" is a writeup on feminism and how, even today, so many women face discrimination for the simple fact that they are women. This essay is co-written by Syna and Mahua.

"Write Your Own Story" is based on a girl with a vast imagination and loves anything fictional.

**Yashashvi Arya**

Yashashvi Arya is an average sixteen-year-old. Her hobbies change frequently, but they are always a medium in which she can express her creative self. She wants to keep trying new things in order to push herself out of her comfort zone and build confidence since she has none. Writing this poem was a part of the same.

The poem 'Keychain' was written with the intention to provide some food for thought, so that the readers can come up with their own stories to explain it. The poem can be interpreted as a mental diary of an introvert, who is struggling with their feelings regarding a special someone. Is it their infatuation that they are hiding, or is it something else?

You can write to her on yashashvi.arya@gmail.com

**Prateek Sibal**

Prateek Sibal is a seventeen-year-old boy who is studying at St. Mary's Junior College, Pune. He has enjoyed writing ever since he was a child and is an avid reader. Prateek loves playing the piano and listening to music, and is very interested in biology and the eccentricities of living things.

'Inheritance' is a short story which deals with several issues including loss and grief. It has hardly been a year since Charlotte Green lost her mother, and as she stands where her mother once stood, we see her memories come flooding back. She is now at a crossroads – the results of a medical test decide the path that she will take, and her life, quite literally, hangs in the balance.

**Dev Gala**

Dev is a sixteen-year-old boy who aspires to be a clinical psychologist and finds his therapy in writing. The movie 'Dead Poets Society' is a huge source of literary inspiration to him. He usually writes about his chaotic emotions and expresses them through words. He also expresses himself through food. He enjoys baking and is usually found recreating dishes from old pastry chefs' recipes. In addition, he loves to swim and continues to do so, ever since he was five. You can write to him at devgala28@gmail.com.

**Advaya Venbakkam**

Advaya is a seventeen-year-old who is currently studying at The Orbis School, Pune. She draws her inspiration for writing from her personal experiences as well as sad music. She enjoys reading, playing the piano, painting and coding and would love to become a professional coder one day.

'Run!' is a story set in a fantasy world. It tells the tale of how a high school girl, after an especially bad month, ends up in a new and terrifying place and has to face her monster to finally be free. You can write to her at advaya.venbakkam@gmail.com.

**Sharvari Choudhari**

Sharvari Choudhari is a sixteen-year-old girl who is fascinated by our universe and loves astronomy. She is an avid writer as well as a passionate singer-songwriter. She plays the guitar, the piano and is also a talented photographer and painter. She believes that little acts of kindness make a difference in the world. Inspired by the women in science, she wishes to continue to unravel the mysteries of science and become a scientist in the future.

You can contact her on s.sharvari.choudhari@gmail.com

**Diya Jadhav**

Diya is a seventeen-year-old girl who is currently studying at Air Force School, Pune. She has no particular inclination towards writing but found it a way to pen her thoughts down. Her hobbies include reading and painting. She aspires to be an entrepreneur.

"Closer to life" explores the numerous joys that nature gives us but which go unnoticed under the tensions of the fast-paced world. It is a peek into a city kid's holiday in his hometown.

You can write to her at jadhav.sonali.arjun@gmail.com

**Diya Jain**

Diya Jain is a seventeen-year-old girl currently studying science in Fergusson College, Pune. She's been a voracious reader from a very young age, she says, "I'm very thankful to my dad who started reading to me before I slept when I was a child; all my inspiration for reading books comes from him." She has written about sixty poems on various topics ranging from death to nature and sad broken hearts to happiness. Writing has always been a sort of outlet to her where she can openly express herself, clear her mind and get the weight off of her chest. She is really hoping to publish her own anthology of poems one day.

You can write to her at diyajainranu@gmail.com.

**Anusha Malusare**

*"Chaos makes the muse, so find comfort in your chaos."*

Anusha is currently studying in the 12$^{th}$ grade. She's passionate about art and poetry. She aspires to become a designer. Anusha has an interest in dramatics and has completed multiple trinity college exams. Anusha is a mammoth epicure, a second eclectic but also enjoys psychological thrillers. Her work usually draws inspiration from nature and is a retrospection of life. You can write to her at anusha.malusare@gmail.com.

"The Exchange" is a short story taking place in a neighbourhood with a new family that seems normal, but really isn't. The story is another take on the famous rendition story "My last babysitting."

**Saniya Gadhave**

Saniya is a fifteen-year young girl currently studying in Pune. She tends to dwell upon the deeper aspects of adolescence and is also an avid nature lover. Both of these qualities thoughtfully reflect in her poems. She actively tries to help make the world a better place in her own small but significant ways, and aspires to work at the United Nations one day. Leaving aside all the seriousness, Saniya also loves indulging into the funnier aspects of life, and tries making others laugh with her short story. She can be contacted at saniya06.12.05@gmail.com.

**Arushi Walkade**

Arushi is a seventeen-year-old student, studying in Army Public School. While she isn't extremely inclined towards writing stories and books, she does enjoy writing occasional one-part stories on her phone. Arushi says she draws inspiration for character designs from online comics and books she reads. Currently, she is focusing on her studies (since 12th is the board year and all that), but writing comes as a breather into her life at times. Apart from this, she is also a bit of a K-pop buff, something that she is very passionate about. You can connect with Arushi at arushiwalkade@gmail.com.

**Ananya Krishnan**

Ananya Krishnan is seventeen years old, currently studying at St. Mary's Junior College, Pune. She enjoys writing prose and draws inspiration from the music she listens to, including Fall Out Boy, Coldplay, Taylor Swift and Day6. She has a keen interest in design, in which she hopes she can pursue a career.

Ananya donates to various NGOs and humanitarian causes in an effort to live in a world free of discrimination, and hopes that her efforts can make the slightest difference in making the world a better place.